I0822891

Gog:
A Tale of the Last Woodland Gnome

By: Gail McDonald

Table of Contents

Chapter 1
A Gnome's Cottage

In a shady dell, half a distance down a lane that meandered into deep woods, nestled an old stone cottage. Its cedar shake roof was covered with green moss, and grapevines were entwined about its chimney. A wisp of wood smoke snaked its way heavenward and dissipated with the northeast wind. Bronze leaves crackled under the gnome's instep as he hesitated at his thick oaken door . . . and then went in.

Gog took off his brown leather hat that was lined with fur. His wizened features, ugly but intelligent, bespoke a thinker, a woodland philosopher. Gog casually hung his worn and patched jacket upon an exposed angle of the wall. The heat within his cottage walls quickly thawed his aging body, lessening his aches and pains. He closed his eyes and greedily inhaled the aromas of his cooking dinner. Having spent the day splitting and stacking firewood, his hunger attacked him with a vengeance.

The gnome quickly turned his attention to setting the table. Once he had placed his carved, wooden cutlery and cloth napkin on the table, he ladled a generous portion of savory stew into a bowl, arranged biscuits on a plate, and moved a skillet of baked apples to the hearth to cool. He pulled a wobbly, handmade wooden chair to the table and sat down. He immediately bowed his balding gray head in prayer, muttered a blessing, and then reverently began to eat his meal. It felt so good to be home!

Gog frowned slightly when his eyes alighted upon a clear glass bottle with a slender neck that sat kitty corner from him at the end of the table. The bottle sat there, sequestered from the rest of the cottage in its patch of gloom; and it glimmered from within with an unearthly, pulsating green light. When the gnome's eyes fell upon it, his shaggy brows immediately knit together, portraying someone caught up in numerous sorrows.

Late autumn light crept through the lone window, and the bottle seemed to bask in the final illumination of an early November sunset that weakly filtered into the cottage. The bottle itself appeared to have a life of its own; for the green light flickering from within cast eerie shadows in the pool of light around its base, and its origin could have been attributed to a world much beyond the one it which it currently existed.

Gog's eyes were glued to the presence of this green light within the bottle. He sat quietly contemplating its throbbing existence, and only an occasional pop from a few exploding embers in the fireplace disturbed the pervasive silence in his home. The gnome seemed comforted in having the bottle close by, though his eyes soon began to well with tears. One could sense immediately that the bottle was causing him at least as much pain as comfort.

Forcing himself out of his uncomfortable reverie, Gog rose from the table and ambled over to the hearth where he stoked the coals in the fireplace into flame. He tossed two medium-sized dry logs upon the red-hot coals and followed them by another large log, still a bit green; so that the fire, once rekindled, would then simmer with warmth for the long evening ahead. He leaned back away from the dancing sparks that flashed and danced up the chimney, warming his hands at the gold and blue flames that were already licking at the logs. The flames projected new dancing shadows upon the wall and brought renewed life to the cottage's interior. Gog made a concentrated effort to ignore the bottle on his table—at least for the time being.

The heart of Gog's cottage was most definitely his fireplace. It was constructed of fieldstone; and it had a large, raised hearth. Iron tripods held cast iron cauldrons which were used as both ovens and cooking pots. The fireplace provided much needed heat, light, and even entertainment for the gnome. Radiant heat from the field stone pulsed throughout the little house providing warmth while the more flickering flames that heated hearth stones cooked soups and baked bread. A gentle glow bathed the walls of the home with flickering light, and often Gog sat for hours in front of his fireplace, thinking about his life as he stared into its depths. During the bitter cold seasons the fireplace was in constant use, and the flickering flames were the heartbeat of life found in this little home in the forest.

Shadows draped across the corners of the interior of Gog's home. The stump of a beeswax candle flickered on the table as the gnome returned to quietly partake of his meal. A rustic wooden pallet covered with two patchwork quilts and a large, lumpy pillow fit snugly against an outer wall. It was positioned in a corner of the cottage, adjacent to the hearth. The bed was indeed simple and the bedding sparse, yet it met his needs.

The top quilt was a crude assemblage of the furs of rabbit and squirrel. The second quilt was a *memory* quilt, for it contained bits and pieces of fabric from clothes that both his mother and he had worn over the years. Filled with the fluffiest of partridge down and then stitched back together with care, this quilt not only combated the cold but also linked the gnome to his heritage and ancestral ties which were buried deep within these woodlands.

A lonely bench was placed to the side of the hearth and was used for the gnome's convenience when he tended the fire or cooked. A crude open cupboard sat to the left of the hearth, and it contained wooden serving plates and utensils, hardened by age and exhibiting a glossy patina from usage; both the cupboard and utensils had been hand-carved from hardwoods over many years. A dilapidated and dog-eared Good Book was propped on an upper shelf in a place of honor. Down below, a few glass bottles of dandelion and grape wines—along with some empty bottles, were stored on the very bottom shelf.

Herbs and dried flowers dangled from the rafters, and a glimmer of light was just now fading from the solitary window that was located to the right of the back door. Gog's little cottage was simple, and most would probably call it spare, but it suited the gnome's needs. For his comfort, a handmade rocking chair with a seat concocted of a rather ratty quilted pillow graced the area in front of the hearth, keeping a respectable distance from the dancing sparks that flew up the fireplace. He luxuriated in the heat from the fire's glowing embers and inhaled the enticing aromas left over from the simmering stew and baked apples.

Eating was always a lonely business for the gnome, and he knew that being solitary would never bring him the pleasure or fulfillment he often dreamed about. He could provide himself with warmth, fill his belly with food, keep busy with a sense of industry, and read his Good Book. But he could not conjure up another gnome with whom he could share his life. Gog was now the sole occupant of the cottage, and his only pet and companion was a one-winged chickadee that perched sadly in its woven willow-twig cage. Gog looked at the little bird fondly and gently tossed him a few biscuit crumbs.

"Solomon, my little fellow. How be ye today? I've missed your *cheep* this day long. I hope you are not under the weather or ailing?"

The chickadee began to slowly pick away at his crumbs; and then he moved over to the edge of the cage, seemingly to get closer to the voice addressing him. He cocked his head and then managed a cautious, weak-throated "*cheep*" before he resumed picking at his food. He was comforted by Gog's presence, though he too seemed to be immersed in his own loneliness. He gently attempted to flap both his wings, and his *ghost* wing, that wing that dangled useless at his side, felt every bit as real as his mobile, feathered wing—though, sadly, it was not.

The little chickadee despaired, *He knows I cannot speak, and yet he speaks to me as if I can. Perhaps he thinks that someday I might. I wish that could be true. I certainly do. He has such a good heart, and he has been my mainstay for these many years now. But all I can do to acknowledge his presence is to bob my head, chirp, and pick at the food he provides.*

Gog finally returned to studying the bottle on his table once more. It seemed that he had needed to gather his strength to do so. Though it pained him greatly, he could not resist the temptation that its presence offered. He lightly touched the surface of the bottle in awe.

"Selah. My mother," he softly spoke to the presence within. "Your being here provides me the little happiness left me in this lonely world. Your spirit contained within this bottle is with me every day. What solace you provide me!" He lovingly gripped the bottle with both hands and wondered at the mesmerizing light within it. A slight warmth emanated from the bottle, and Gog trembled with pent-up emotion as he realized that it came from his mother's love that continued to pulse with its other-worldly energy.

So much of the happiness remaining in Gog's world seemed indeed to be preserved within this very bottle. Unfortunately, it was a happiness that he had stolen at a time when he had been overcome by desperation. He had made a rather selfish bargain that had allowed him to keep his mother's spirit with him, though it had cost her soul its freedom. This bargain still made Gog feel incredibly guilty to this very day.

"When my mother passed away, I was able to prevent her soul from completing its journey at the very end of her life by capturing it within this bottle just prior to its celestial flight to Heaven. I captured it within the bottle because I was agonizing over my plight of being left all alone in the world upon her death. I had panicked, there's no doubt about it. I could not imagine losing my mother. Perhaps I had just acted selfishly at the time, thinking far more about my own circumstances than my mother's."

"Frightened out of my mind, I could only think about losing the only love and family I had ever known, forever. How could I go on with so little in my world to comfort me? I frantically looked for any solution that might prevent me from experiencing this major loss. My eyes had sought a solution when they had rested upon an empty wine bottle that still retained its cork. My heart began to beat faster, for I was grasping for a miracle, and my imagination was proposing an answer to my desperate prayers. I grabbed the bottle, uncorking it as I caught sideways glimpses of my mother's iridescent soul preparing for flight, and then I quickly approached it. Somehow, I had been able to capture it within the confining glass prison of the bottle, and I immediately corked it so that it could not continue heavenward."

"I am probably the worst of sinners for having done what I did, but at the time I had been unable to envision any life without my mother. The thoughts of her immediate and total departure had brought gloomy visions and darkest thoughts. Any love that I had ever known and experienced would have disappeared like a puff of smoke, and I would be almost totally alone for the rest of my life. Now, I am faced with being unable to forgive myself for having imprisoned my mother's soul at the very moment when it had wished to soar to freedom, to a forever meeting with her Maker. My guilt is unrelenting and lies heavy upon me."

"In spite of my unforgivable deed, it seems that I have been able to go on with my life—cherishing Selah's light-filled, though insubstantial presence. But it is most definitely a far cry from having her with me in a more physical sense as she was when alive and walking this earth. Sometimes I just cannot escape the guilt I feel for having captured her spirit, and I constantly wrestle with the regret that weighs upon me. There are so many times that I wish that I had not acted so impulsively."

"I suppose that I could have chosen to set her spirit free at a much later time, in the hope of seeking forgiveness from my Savior for what I had done. Uncorking the bottle to release her soul might have appeared to be a valiant attempt at trying in a small way to make up for what I had done, but I just couldn't do it! It seems that I have been a total coward in this. Her being with me is far too important now, and it seems that my selfishness has won out—at least for a time. And though I realize I may have risked my own soul in doing what I did, I can but ask for forgiveness in my prayers, from my mother and from my Maker and my Savior. Yet, I realize that in some convoluted way that I did what I felt I had to do—to survive the unbearable reality of losing the only love that provided me with grounding to my woodland home. With Selah's spirit in the bottle, I am not totally alone—and that is what seems to matter the most."

***

Gog was a woodland gnome, a border being of a race which had lost its last stronghold centuries ago. He and his mother had always lived near mankind, but they had never been completely of mankind. Of their ancestors, there no longer remained any trace. They had become but a vestige of what their race had once been—a glorious synergism of nature's man, a lost cousin of Abel, beings who were irrevocably tied to both Heaven and earth.

Only snippets were recorded of these border beings, for they were from a lost race, beings who had lost their race; border beings—living on the very edge of civilization, boarder beings—existing within the world but not fully owning it; strangers from before the dawn of time, stranger than mankind; timeless as time is meaningless, timeless as—sadly, little time remains. Be that as it may, Gog was the last of a proud race. Nonetheless, he was the very last; and in that he was continually buffeted by the winds of desolation.

Gog was not a beautiful being. He was earthy. He had a swarthy nut-brown complexion with a myriad of wrinkles, graying hair, high cheekbones, full lips, and a grizzled beard. He had an intelligent high forehead, complex hazel eyes, and inappropriate elephantine ears. A dimpled chin winked through his beard, and his head rested on no perceivable neck—all in all a rather pitiful example of what it is to be a gnome. Yet, unbelievably, whenever any creature first saw Gog, pleasure was all that was felt. Love, warmth, and kindness emanated from this gentle being.

Gog knew that his true gifts were not of a physical nature, they came from within— his intellect, imagination, and compassion were what distinguished him. His love and kindness were the true treasures of his soul. Often, his most innermost thoughts needed to be expressed, and only language that could paint a picture or tell a story would do. As a poet, he would sometimes attempt to mingle the everyday world with the worlds he could only imagine. He was often humbled by a kind of celestial music that sometimes seemed to accompany the beauty and imagery of his words.

A flash of dazzlement,
A brilliant beam of intellect mirrored from heaven on high—
Kissing, for just an instant, the Universe.
A flash of brilliance,
A creative spark that kindles light,
Too soon lost in the eternity of sighs.

Gog's poetry was composed of a wide variety of thoughts that had once glimmered in his mind like quicksilver, words just waiting for their opportunity to exist. The gnome was philosophical in his approach to life and spiritual in his beliefs. Creating poetry was his most precious pleasure, for it mirrored his translation of life—along with his many hopes and dreams. His thoughts were deep, and they often wandered, sometimes becoming a bit obscure until they finally emerged with a sense of clarity and purpose. Quite often, however, his poetry spoke of the preciousness of life, especially as is found in the natural world. Poetry was the song of his life.

As Gog sat by his doorway pondering life, sometimes watching the struggles of the very smallest of creatures, he would gently say, "I would like to think that if a beetle were to scuttle across my threshold that I would as gladly let it in as let it out." He revered life in all its shapes, forms, and nuances. The beauty of existence in the world around him was truly a miracle to behold. He felt himself blessed.

***

For the gnome, life in the wooded dell was not strictly measured in years. Gog couldn't say whether he had lived years, decades, or centuries. The seasons came in waves and lapped at the edge of the forest. Passing time was marked in plantings, harvests, and contemplation.

The senses experienced the passage of time through the varied parade of seasons. The gnome's sense of smell scanned the progression of the seasons, reminding him of spring's fragrances of rain-drenched earth, summer's pungent green onions, fall's ferny woodland paths strewn with leaves, and the hot, winter's steaming wet wool on a hot hearth. His taste buds savored the spring flavors of bitter dandelion greens, summer's tangy red tomatoes, fall's sweet wildflower honey, and wintry juicy wild apples. His eyes feasted upon the parading beauty of curled fiddleheads in the spring, iridescent dragonflies on a summer's day, a brilliant red cardinal on an autumn bough, and glistening icicles in a wintry beam of sunlight. His wrinkled skin tingled as it absorbed spring's warm raindrops, scalding summer sun, autumn's chill drafts, and the icy sleet of winter. And his very ears trembled in delight to the music of melodic redwings in a spring marsh, droning mosquitoes in summer's glen, crisp leaves rattling in a fall gust , and the moaning of winter winds. The natural world surrounded him with its presence, and Gog embraced it as it wended its way through season after season, year after year.

The beauty and timelessness of the natural world often held Gog spellbound. In awe, he witnessed the sun setting with the backdrop of a cloudless sky—drenched in peach and mauve. He saw the moon rise, sometimes silver and sometimes gold with twinkling stars etched across the night. Clouds often scudded across the sky, obliterating the heavenly light for a time; and Gog often gave witness to the viciously slanting raindrops that dramatically beat upon the soil as well as to the gently floating snowflakes that fell to earth in a cloud of white as soft as feathers. New, tender creatures came into the world; and sick, sometimes aged creatures left it. The seasons passed in a knowable progression with the gnome spending much of his time on both toil and reflection. The world went on—time passed. And Gog's life continued towards tomorrow.

Chapter 2
Remembering Selah

Gog had no precise way of keeping track of time, nor did he have any inclination to do so. A rather ancient grandfather clock was nestled in a corner by his front door, but it provided ambiance and perhaps a link to the distant past more than anything else. He had never depended upon it as a timekeeper. The old, dilapidated clock continued to tick, and its pendulum swung right and left laboriously as the hours were counted off in a rather lackadaisical fashion. Gog kept the clock's mechanism wound with a rusty old key, and it continued to report the passing of each hour—just as it seems it had forever. He could never verify its accuracy, but it could be depended upon to keep him company during many a long winter's night.

It's true that Gog did not have the type of schedule that required the precision of a clock to announce the hours of the day; but he had to admit that its ticking and chiming provided him with that measure of comfort and stability in his world. It gave him a sense of the progression of time in a world that had always relied upon its own schedule based on the sun, the moon, and the ocean tides. But the percussive tick-tocks and the rather anemic tonality of its chimes provided his home with a sweet music all its own.

Gog had never owned a calendar, his interest in the hours on the face of the clock in relationship to the position of its hands was fleeting at best, and the distant church bells that he sometimes heard when the atmosphere was just right never helped to make the Sabbath any more of a reality to him just because the outside world proclaimed that it was Sunday. Still, Gog knew that time was something that existed, and he also knew that it was something that could not be tampered with for anyone's advantage. However, within his own little world, it did provide him with but a fleeting sense of reality that reached beyond his own existence.

When Selah, his mother, had died—the actual timing of this horrific event very probably had not seemed terribly relevant to him then, or indeed ever. His aching heart told him it had been but a month or two ago, though his rational mind told him it had most certainly been many seasons, most probably years, and maybe even an entire decade. He did know it had taken place far too many harvests back, and the ache remained like a glowing coal within him. He never forgot what his mother's presence had meant to him, and he continued to grieve her absence in his life. He remembered her last day when she had softly called him to her side.

"Gog, you know my time is short. My love for you, my only son, is the only tonic that preserved my life for as long as it has. The time for our final parting has finally come, and I can ignore it no longer. Heaven will not continue to keep putting it off. I feel my heart swell with pain as I face our separation. But I refuse to say a final good-bye, for I know we are destined to meet again one day. Our reunion will be sweet and filled with the song of angels, and it will seem that our final parting lasted but a moment. The eternity we will eventually share together will be sweet, and our love and the love of God and his Son will surround us forever."

The mother of Gog possessed beautiful, soft yellow-gray hair, which was now spread across her pillow. Selah smelled of the hearth, herbs and spices, the woods, and the loamy soil of her garden. Her face, wrinkled with age and darkened by the sun, reminded Gog of an autumn nut ready for harvest. Her dark eyes were deep with emotion and age, and her lips whispered condolences and blessings even as she struggled with the discomfort of her own dying.

"My mother was so very dear to me," Gog mumbled in his anguish as he remembered her passing. "I did not want to believe that she would have to leave me alone in a world that already felt too cold and lonely. I refused to acknowledge her farewell. Though I kissed her gently on her cool, dry cheeks— memorizing these most special of loving imprints, I could not accept the finality of her departure. I felt myself beginning to shatter from within, my face began to crumble, and I quickly turned away so that my mother would not see the tears running down my cheeks. Her own suffering in dying was more than enough for her to bear."

Gog knew that Selah undoubtedly didn't want to leave him, alone and bereft without another living soul, but it could not be helped. But, when he saw her life essence flicker and begin its escape, he had immediately panicked. In despair and without a moment's hesitation—he grasped an empty wine bottle and immediately captured her spirit within it. And then, he had quickly corked it tightly to prevent its escape, just as a small child might capture and imprison a lightning bug in a jar. These thoughts and deeds and would hound him unceasingly for as long as he lived.

At the time, however, he had immediately felt grief, guilt, and utter desolation upon carrying out this mission; but he had to admit, even if it was only to himself, he had also experienced a tremendous sense of relief. He tried to totally rationalize away his feelings of guilt and betrayal because, after all, his mother was everything to him—just as he was to her. He thought of his action in preserving her spirit in the bottle as the final loving gesture of a son who was determined to prevent his mother from entering eternity without him—though many times he had trouble convincing himself of the rightness of his action. He wondered if his selfishness might now be construed as an unforgivable sin.

Gog had truly believed at the time that he could not survive alone without his mother. She was all he had ever known of love, and he could not envision himself continuing to exist in a world totally devoid of love. Gog thought he knew that his mother would understand—that his Savior would forgive him. Or so he prayed.

Selah's spiritual essence now shimmered green within the bottle, and Gog was guiltily comforted by her presence. Though her very soul had emerged from her physical body so that it might leave its empty husk behind in Gog's world, still it pulsed with the eternal life that should have been relegated to its new home in the celestial. The gnome knew that he had forced it to remain behind in relative limbo, trapped within a cold bottle where no escape existed, sitting on a table in a place where she had dined much of her life on earth.

Gog, sometimes feeling tremors of shame, attempted to reconcile his actions as he planned a reconciliation of sorts, "One day, when I feel my own life's essence is preparing to vacate my twisted body, I will most certainly set Selah's spirit free, so that together we may soar towards Heaven. Her prolonged stay here on earth is but a bump in the road on her journey to the eternity we will share together, barely a brief hesitation recorded by the hands of time. Our eventual departure will give testament to the resiliency of our souls and their need for completion in our heavenly home which has been prepared for us. We will eventually be together, forever, connected by the everlasting love we share."

At least that was what Gog told himself and how he planned his redemption. He certainly hoped and prayed that his mother and his Maker would forgive him, and that what he had done would not be viewed as totally unpardonable. Gog knew he had done it based on a deep and abiding love for his mother, but he had to admit that his own loneliness had played the larger role in his hasty decision. For now, he'd suck on his empty pipe, sip his dandelion wine, and listen to the sputter of the candle on the sill. The essence of his mother Selah would stay close by—flickering in her bottle.

***

The day following Selah's death, Gog had buried his mother's physical remains in a simple grave that he had carved out of the forest mold deep within the woods. He had first filled her grave with a soft layer of colorful autumn leaves. Then he had lowered her pine coffin into the grave. Only when he saw the stark physical presence of the coffin, nestled in its almost-gaudy bed of red and orange leaves, did he fully realize the loss of her physical presence. Before closing the coffin, he had gently placed her hands in an attitude of prayer and then kissed her ice-cold cheeks. He knew without a doubt that he was the one who needed the prayers, for he truly felt himself to be the very worst of sinners.

"Shoveling the damp earth so that it gently rained down upon her coffin had been the most agonizing part. My very heart rebelled, and for the longest time I thought that I absolutely would not be able to complete my task. Tears poured down upon my cheeks, and sobs shook my entire body. Had I been in the company of another mortal being, I might have been mistaken for a mad man. Knowing that I could not avoid my task and realizing that I must honor Selah's body with a proper burial, I continued with the heartbreaking deed until it was done. Soon nothing remained but the forest soil and a deep silence that was heavy as sin."

Gog had bowed his head and honored his mother's absence with song and prayers. His prayers had been heartfelt but barely audible, as he had proclaimed all her loving attributes in a petition for her acceptance into an everlasting realm. When he realized his petition would fall on deaf ears because he himself had prevented her soul's entry into Heaven, he shivered with dread and remorse. He knew that his ceremony was far too superficial and false, most definitely lacking in God's approval. He found himself torn between what he knew his Maker would most certainly have decreed and what he felt was the only option for his own survival in a world that had lost the last vestiges of his mother's love. But what was done was done. Burdened with so much loss, he turned his back on Selah's gravesite and returned to his cottage.

Gog eventually rolled a large boulder to sit at the head of Selah's grave. The stone had been carefully chiseled with an epitaph—*SELAH, beloved mother of Gog.* Gog stared at his carvings on the boulder's flat front surface, and he knew that these words were also chiseled upon his heart. He had placed a bottle of goldenrod in front of the stone, and in the days to come he left fresh flowers or colorful branches of leaves from time to time to honor her. In all that really mattered, Gog knew that nothing of any true value remained in his mother's grave; but it was important that he remember where her body lay in repose so that from time to time he could visit this hallowed ground and leave his gifts of nature—tokens that might be deemed a small part of his penance. He knew that in some way it might also provide him meager comfort as well.

"My conscience greatly troubles me now for, though my mother's body reposes in eternal sleep, *ashes to ashes and dust to dust*, her spirit still throbs with light and vitality beside my hearth—having been imprisoned in a bottle by my own hand. What will my graveside prayers amount to when I have not allowed her soul to depart to its eternity where she should now be residing with her Maker."

Unfortunately, though the guilt was eating Gog alive, he was still unable to accept a world totally devoid of his mother's presence. Things would remain as they were.

"I hope and pray that my Savior's forgiveness is possible, for he is undeniably the light of the world. And it is only through my Maker's blessing will I have any hope of an eternal life. Selah will surely forgive me. She will always be my mother, and I pray that a mother's love is endless. I do know that I am totally bereft without her; and, without her spirit's presence, I would be totally lost in a very lonely world."

***

Over the years of residing with Selah in their woodland habitat, Gog, like most children, had taken his mother's presence for granted. She had always been there for him, and her love had been as free-flowing as the stream through the glen or the oxygen in the air—all necessary in sustaining his life. Gog's mother had cooked and cleaned for the pair of them. She had put up preserves, tended the garden, made candles, mended and sewn, and maintained the hearth. But, more than that, she had always been there for him emotionally as well. She had showered him with affection, shown abundantly by her many hugs and kisses. She praised him when praise was deserved, chastised him when necessary; and comforted him with her forgiveness after her disfavor had run its course. She had diligently made their cottage a loving home.

Selah had also provided her son with a buffer against the outside world. As the last two living woodland gnomes, she had created a sense of normalcy for him. She had provided a loving environment that had encouraged his strengths and forgiven his weaknesses. Gog's mother had been his guardian and spiritual guide in a world that could be both cold and cruel. Her loving arms had wrapped him in security, stability, and serenity. As a woman of faith, Selah had given him his belief system and nurtured his spirituality. She had provided him with that *someone else* into whose eyes he could gaze so that he could read another interpretation of the world.

Gog frowned with the knowledge of realizing too late what he had lost. "I never questioned my life with my mother for even a moment. I had unrealistically believed that it would go on and on—forever. Her life and my life together were all I had ever known, and I had never been given any reason to believe that an ending would ever have to come. No, of course it was not logical; but it was what I believed, what I wished and hoped for."

"And, of course, I certainly had no real knowledge of death. I had never experienced it except in the few sacrifices of the animals that sustained us and in the few woodland creatures that we had seen succumb to it on occasion. We appreciated, revered, and respected these little forest souls that were separate from us but close to us; but we never truly loved them, not as we loved one another. And there is a very real difference." Gog paused a moment, watching a small spider toil at making her web, the delicate weaving fluttering in the gentle breeze that swept his doorstep. When she noticed Gog's presence she scuttled away, disappearing into a deep crack in the door casing.

"When I spent my day tilling the soil, chopping wood, or seeking food in the forest, I always came home knowing that my mother would be there waiting to greet me with outstretched arms. And she always was. I was dependent upon her for so much, and I never questioned how God's plans would play a decisive role in our lives as He determined the many different paths that we would be forced to take along the way. I know now that I was naïve beyond belief. But because of this innocence, I suppose that my childhood was filled with even more sunshine and happiness—for I was never aware of the uncertainties that could lead to fear. I never knew that there was a lurking Darkness that existed for all mortals—a presence that many of us come to deem as Oblivion, that but waits to pounce, attempting to destroy much of the happiness in our lives."

With Selah's passing, Gog had chosen to arm wrestle with his fate to maintain his claim on his mother's soul, so that he would not have to be so totally alone. Capturing her soul within a corked bottle was nothing more than an empty victory, for the real Selah—though perhaps with him in spirit—was indeed just a mirage of what she had once been. Her bottled presence was the barest of reflections, possessing but a mere glimmer of her true light, reducing her to a mute prisoner who no longer claimed full residency in the realm of life.

Though Gog had deluded himself into believing that his life was better with his mother's captured soul than without her at all, he had—in fact—made his life far more tragic. He now lived with the guilt of what he had done, her memory was quietly fading though her spirit remained, and he was unable to fully grieve his loss so that he could emotionally recover from her physical death. He could not totally move forward in his life because, not only had he imprisoned her soul to offer himself some consolation, but he had also preserved much of the sorrow he had felt upon her physical death.

Gog could continue to enjoy his life, but it came with a penalty. He would anticipate the day when he could release his mother's spirit when it was his turn to seek God in His Heaven, but he would remain clueless as to when that would be. He knew that their simultaneous releases would probably be the only way in which he could ever free himself from the guilt that surrounded him, to finally feel true peace and joy once more. He hoped to free his mother so that she could seek her salvation, and he most desperately wanted to accompany her on this journey to the all-encompassing Light that would replace all that they had come to know in the woodlands.

Chapter 3
Life Goes On

The woods were more home to Gog than his own cottage. The season didn't matter; hot or cold, the woods held mystery and life's lessons. Creation had applied both art and science to build a world of beauty with a sense of order, and now Gog was present as a totally absorbed student and observer. Sometimes, entranced, he'd spend hours watching the gradual disappearance of a crystalline icicle as it slowly diminished, droplet by droplet, reflecting the colors of light in its glowing prism. One day, studying a toadstool that had been but spore days before, he marveled at its microcosmic birth as it grew upward from the forest floor—quickly taking shape and form, eventually sporting a nut-brown overcoat and orange-red fluted throat. Life in all its preciousness, varieties and species, delighted him. He could not totally understand it, however. He could not begin to understand it!

"Life. Now that is an ongoing puzzle. Sometimes its preciousness almost makes me choke-up with emotions because I am so powerless to fully describe or understand these marvels that God has created—from the largest, most majestic to the smallest, least significant. Though I know that in God's eyes even the seemingly least significant becomes incredibly significant because it too has a role to play on earth and is important beyond all measure. Even the ordinary becomes extraordinary if I but take the time to examine and imagine all that exists within and without its reality."

When Gog set off on his many jaunts, he savored the time he spent ambling through the woodlands, and his curiosity never wavered. "Things do more than take up space. They shimmer and throb with an inner light of their very own. Things have spirits, I know it. Maybe not rocks or wind or water; they are but containers. But trees and birds and all things made of living matter have that spark of life. They pulse with warmth, an eternal breath and significance, for all are my Maker's creations."

There was his own life. His mother, when alive, had told him in more than words that he was her treasure of a lifetime. He was precious in her eyes, her love was unconditional, and the world was a far better place for their relationship. But in this love's strength was also fragility, the irony of life. Things this perfect were never meant to last forever. Gog, the poet, had remembered his mother in verse,

The bush of a yellow rose struggles in the pale October sun
to bloom at least one last time.
Blasted by a savage frost,
it holds on to the hope of one more perfect bloom.
The sun is gentle, benign, encouraging—
but it offers no lasting protection
from the nightfall's harsh rampage—the final killer frost.
Still, the rose lifts its fragile stem and basks in the sun
with hope.
What else can it do?

Gog thought often of his mother, their close relationship, and the sadness that now existed for him in his loneliness. His true measure of comfort seemed to come from the green glimmer of his mother's soul, a physical reminder of something precious that had once existed, a flickering green glow that continued to remind Gog of his precious Selah. Salty tears fell from his cloudy brown eyes from time to time when he remembered his loss, yet it seemed that the natural world around him remained persistent in providing him with purpose, beauty, and pleasure. There always seemed to be a new sense of joy in the mysteries displayed in the wooded glen, blessings provided by the gifts it presented, and a sense of peace found there as he traveled its many paths.

Though his world seemed not quite so familiar as the world which he and his mother had once shared together, still it continued to throb with life and renewal. Though it sometimes seemed to be more a place of emptiness and shadows, and the chill wind tended to blow stronger now and the sunshine seemed less intense from his loss, his woodland home gradually began to speak to him of happiness, contentment, and a belief in a brighter tomorrow.

And so, though the gnome continued to carry his burden of sorrow, he came to realize that hope was something that never truly died. As lonely and as miserable as Gog sometimes felt, he never gave up on praying for a better tomorrow . . . praying that someday he would reconcile himself to his loss, and that his future would bring his mother and himself together again in spirit—forever. He decided that his Maker would want him to continue seeking joy, beauty, and the many simple pleasures that existed in his woodland home.

Gog found that he was able to fill his loving heart and mind with the many blessings that he found all around him in nature. He tramped through his woods—easily discovering the marvels of a natural world that provided him with many lessons: beauty, inspiration, endurance, birth, and growth. He was fascinated to learn which blossoms attracted the honey bees, awestruck when the dogwood and mountain laurel painted his woods with bloom, mesmerized by the lunar eclipse that blanketed his world in silver, and enchanted by the strutting of a turkey gobbler with his full tail of feathers on display as he sought his mate. Timing was always of the essence in these things, so the gnome was always vigilant.

Gog learned that patience was indeed a virtue, so if he came upon a small miracle which might have only just begun to take place, he took it in stride—and patiently waited for its completion. When he noticed that the marsh marigolds in the swampland were just starting to bud, he simply picked a basketful of their greens and brought them home to simmer for his supper; and then he returned a few days later to enjoy the brilliant yellow of their flowers when they finally burst into bloom—bringing home a large, beautiful bouquet of them for his dining table.

Gog concentrated on spring's colorful display of leaves and buds. He enjoyed the rich colors of the many leaves and flowers that were constantly taking their place in the springtime parade: from the tender red leaves of the maple, to the flowering white explosion of the shad trees, the fragile bloom of the dark red wake-robins that dotted his path, followed by the vivid displays of dogtooth violets and mayflowers, and concluding with spring's finale of the breathtaking multiflora rose—which saturated the approaching summer's air with perfume. So many, many times in springtime, Gog's spirit seemed overwhelmed by the magnificence of the colors and fragrances that were all around him in the woodlands; and it was never long before the forest and clearings were humming with bees, wasps, dragonflies, and butterflies.

"Though there is much to be learned by watching nature all around me when I travel the breadth of my little kingdom, I think that oftentimes it is the sounds that I first notice in the spring. I enjoy hearing my very first male robin after a lengthy bleak winter.

Often, he is looking for his first worm of the season—and sometimes battles a world where snow and ice may continue to hold reign for many days. He must arrive early to select a nesting site for his mate, and because of this too often he must suffer through bitter weather as he patiently awaits her arrival."

Gog smiled as he continued to reminisce, "The chorus of peepers in the swamp is always music to my ears. Often, they are soon joined by the tree frog's vocals. When the redwing blackbird serenades me from the stand of pussy willows, I am filled with happiness; and it is then that I know that spring is finally here to stay. And when the choir of the many birds who have come to these woods to nest and raise families break forth in song at dawn, my old heart truly beats with joy."

Gog knew that spring was often his greatest delight, knowing full well that it was mostly because it followed closely upon the heels of the stark, deep, dark days of the ponderous winter months that came before it. But as he aged and grew in wisdom, he knew that it was important to look for the magic that could be found in all seasons—especially if he chose to keep an open mind and remain alert for the subtle revelations that took place all around him—whatever the season.

"I enjoy seeing a glimmer of the miraculous, the quiet beauty that often exists in much of nature, the precious little daily events, and the drama of new life that unfolds every day. I hope never to get caught up in boredom when the world is filled with so much beauty that can stir the soul. I know that my restless nature seeks delight, and knowledge, and a deeper connection to the world around me."

There were incredible small miracles that took place every spring, and Gog was adept at finding them. One spring a pair of brown wrens took over the hanging potted fern next to Gog's back-door stoop. Standing on an overturned bucket, he could see a miniature nest tucked within the fern, cradling three dainty, speckled eggs. The industrious wrens hatched their chicks, fed them, and then encouraged their brood to take wing long before many of the other birds had even begun to make nesting plans. The gnome had rejoiced in their successful hatch of three, and when he later saw them chasing bugs in his garden, with their jaunty tipped-up tail and joyous song, he couldn't help but smile.

"In the spring I never set out to plan my meals because I am always on the lookout for something fresh and tasty from the woodlands and fields around me. I have enjoyed fried trout with fresh dandelion greens, a partridge stuffed with stray asparagus and wild grains, a goose egg simmered with fiddleheads, and fried dried apples mixed in a fresh watercress salad. Nature's abundance is remarkable, and I always savor the freshness and delicate taste of my meals during this time of year."

Spring was also the time of year when Gog began to shed his winter clothes and bedding. On wash day he soaked these heavier items with his weekly change of clothing in the nearby spring, beating his clothes and bedding on a rock and then hanging them to dry on an ancient oak with low-hanging branches. It was never long before the fragrant breezes and freshening rays of the sun dried the winter's bedding for another season, and his own wash became crisp and clean. Gog, who then thoroughly bathed in the spring himself, used some of the rich clay from the bottom of the spring mixed with a fistful of mint as cleansers. He always thoroughly rinsed himself with the waters of the babbling brook that filled the spring and then lazed on a grassy knoll to allow the brilliant sun's warmth to dry his body and his hair. When he finally dressed himself in his fragrant, newly-washed clothing, he felt like a king.

In spring, Gog always knew that the time was right to overhaul his own appearance and make important changes. Using a well-sharpened knife, he trimmed his beard and hair, decorating a nearby shrub with his discarded locks in the hope that some little songbird might choose to line its nest with their cozy softness. Gog combed his shortened hair and beard with his fingertips, brushed his remaining teeth with spearmint and a bristly twig, and pared his fingernails and toenails with his knife. Looking at the still reflection of himself in the pool, he grinned. He could feel some of his youthfulness return as he discarded those things that had begun to weigh him down over the long winter months. There was no doubt that spring filled him with the spirit of a child, and he rejoiced as he felt it coursing through his veins once again.

Soon the gnome sat on a stool in the shade, industriously fashioning new moccasins from the leather he had prepared over the winter. Though he often went barefoot over much of the spring and summer, it was important to have a decent pair of shoes at his disposal for bad weather and the cooler seasons that were biding their time before making their presence known. He stroked the soft leather, realizing what a luxury it was, and he offered up thanks for the comfort and warmth that it would provide once it was transformed into new footwear.

He inhaled deeply. "Ah, me—I absolutely love the newness of spring and feel that all beginnings are possible at this time of year. Everything is refreshed by the sun, the rain, and the breezes. The smells are so fragrant and ever-changing, and they bring me untold delight. I can almost see the trees, bushes, and plants growing as I make my daily treks through the woodland. The fragrances of the flowers, mellowing soil, and sweet grasses are heavenly; and I thoroughly delight in them because I know that they won't last forever. The songs of the birds inspire my imagination to wander, and my daydreaming brings me so much pleasure. I cannot help but touch the soft petals of the wood geranium, stroke the bark of a towering hickory, or rub the witch hazel leaves between my fingers to release their scent.

"I have most definitely fallen in love with this old world once again, for it seems to have been totally reborn. Rebirth! Joy! Forgiveness! New life! Spring is always a reminder and celebration of Easter. Knowing that my Savior has risen, lives forever, and has forgiven my sins makes me shudder with both happiness and ecstasy. However, it also revives the deep remorse I feel for my own sins. I am so blessed, and yet I feel equally cursed by my very own selfish actions of the past. I have not allowed my own beloved mother to rise from the dead."

Chapter 4
Selah's Tale And Gog Carries On

Many, many moons ago, when Gog's mother had been little more than a young bride herself and Gog was but a baby, the wooded glade had reluctantly parted, allowing an itinerant preacher who was also a peddler by trade to enter the secretive glen. Selah had never questioned the purpose of his arrival after so many years of living in solitude. She was curious, lonely, and trusting. She had not concerned herself with where he might have come from, nor his purpose in showing up on her doorstep at this time. The superstitions and folklore with which she herself had been raised accepted this traveler as someone who had just been blown in by the wind, another marvel of nature, or an interesting interruption in her life like a gentle rain or a cooling breeze. Little did she know that the traveler's visit would irrevocably change her life—like a ferocious blizzard, a dramatic thunderstorm, or an over-brilliant rainbow.

The man wore robes constructed of age-worn woven cotton which had once been died a deep nut brown. They were rather ragged and torn but provided him scant protection from the elements. He wore a canvas cape of an indeterminate color that rode negligently upon his shoulders to combat wind and rain. He navigated the well-traveled paths, using his staff to negotiate the twists and bends, carrying a load of books in a knapsack upon his back. A huge and rather scroungy dog followed close upon his heels, pulling a small cart that seemed to be constructed more like a sled with center wheels.

It was overloaded with various sundries and utensils. He wore his white hair and beard extravagantly long—both masses of hair braided to avoid the tangles he met as he thrashed through the underbrush of wild berry bushes and thorn apple. And his pathetic brown dog's coat seemed to be composed of far more stickers, thorns, and clinging branches than fur—making him appear even larger than he really was.

Selah had welcomed the lonely traveler to her woodland home, sharing the meager refreshments that she had on hand, and he had remained with Gog and his mother for seven days—with her permission, setting up his camp 100 paces from their small cottage. He had positioned a tripod above a miserly campfire that he had quickly constructed with the rocks and scattered branches found on the forest floor. He soon introduced a kettle to the mix for his bathing and the sporadic cup of tea, and then proceeded to live off the land with what he could scrounge from the forest, thankfully augmenting it with Selah's kindness as she donated countless scoops of herbal tea, cups of porridge and soup, and numerous batches of biscuits accompanied by honey combs.

The man had fashioned a makeshift roof of pine boughs laid upon a skeleton frame of ash limbs to establish a temporary shelter, and he had then laid additional pine boughs upon the forest floor beneath his structure, pine boughs redolent with the fragrance of pitch. The boughs, mingled with scattered dead leaves, moss, and lichens created a bed of sorts in his humble abode.

The stranger never gave his name, so Selah had decided to address him as *"Mr. Traveling Man."* And, though she had carefully introduced herself, Gog at that point—being but a wee babe yet unnamed—the man had quickly gotten in the habit of calling them nothing more than *Mother* and *Child*. He was respectful, kind, and had no wishes to invade their privacy in the woodland. Before long Selah realized that she was thoroughly enjoying this strange man's unanticipated visit.

On the very first day of Mr. Traveling Man's visit, Selah and her child were introduced to the vast array of tinker treasures from the cart: a collection of utensils and sundries which were certainly not available in the wilds of the forest. Selah, a most wonderful homemaker, had been mesmerized by the many articles for sale. She set aside a selection of them for herself, knowing that they would make doing her chores easier and more efficient, choosing each one carefully and wisely. Soon she was indebted to the visitor for two large tin cups for soup and tea, a very large metal spoon, wool and corduroy fabric, a roll of twine, very large scissors, a paring knife and butcher knife, two large woolen hats, and a wooden mixing bowl—her list gradually grew each day that the peddler remained. She was always practical, never extravagant, in each of her selections.

"Of course, I did not have coin with which to pay for my numerous purchases, but Mr. Traveling Man encouraged me nonetheless to shop, amicably agreeing to barter with me for the wares in which I showed interest. I did possess woodland treasures of my own, some of which I had in excess—items that were of bartering interest to Mr. Traveling Man for his own use or that for his future customers: honeycombs, pouches of black walnuts and hazelnuts, strings of dried apples, a jug of elderberry wine, packets of herbs, polished moonstones; cakes of maple sugar, and figurines hand-carved from polished maple wood and pine. These were friendly transactions, and Mr. Traveling Man and I concluded our bartering in due time, both of us satisfied with what we had swapped with one another."

Selah had kindly curried the poor dog's matted fur, bathed him in the brook, brushed him until his coat shown glossy with care, then trimmed it close for comfort. She had fed him scraps from the soup pot and gifted him with his very own soup bone. She had also taken it upon herself to do Mr. Traveling Man's laundry and repacked his cart so his purchases would travel more easily when he left. For all her kindnesses, Mr. Traveling Man gifted Selah with a thimble, a packet of needles and thread; knitting needles and yarn; scraps of fabric; and an old shawl that had begun to unravel— though it still retained its color and warmth and could easily be repaired. She was delighted with her gifts while Mr. Traveling Man was convinced that he, in fact, had received the best of the deal.

One morning Mr. Traveling Man invited Selah and her babe to his own modest fireside. He gave her a mug of tea and the child a sweetened teething chew, and then he seriously began to introduce her to faith. Many years later, Selah still remembered this visit as if it had happened yesterday.

"After we took our seats, he explained that he was going to take us on a journey; and, hopefully, at the very end of it—we might be fortunate enough to find ourselves at a wonderful destination. He prayed that I would find *Faith*. But I would truly have to open my heart and my mind to God and my Savior Jesus Christ, so that I could find this thing that was more precious than all the riches in the world."

"I was a bit bewildered by Mr. Traveling Man's compassionate pitch for something that could not be seen, nor easily understood. Faith was not an elixir, or a new tool, or a creative verse in a book. It didn't solve day-to-day problems, entertain, or provide physical comfort. But it demonstrated unconditional love, changed lives, and gave hope in abundance. The importance of Faith was still a total mystery to me, and yet the man's loving persuasiveness encouraged me to imagine how Faith could become a major motivation in my own life, even here in the seclusion of my woodland home."

Then Mr. Traveling Man removed a large book from his satchel and, carefully opening it with much ceremony, spreading it out upon his knees. With his sonorous and mellow voice, he began to read and discuss the wondrous stories found within it. He called it **The *Good Book***, and for more than three hours he held Selah spellbound as he began to reveal the magic, the pathos, the joy and the tragedy, and the all-encompassing love that was contained within it.

"His voice droned on and on into the stillness of the day, even after our break for the noonday meal. Most importantly, he introduced me to God and Jesus. He taught me about thanking God, my Maker, for our blessings at every meal. He taught me about prayer. He opened my heart to a blossoming that I felt was changing me forever for the good. As my child slept soundly; I was mesmerized, intent in soaking up every nuance of **The Good Book's** many messages, memorizing storylines, feeling the passion, and knowing without a doubt that I had been touched by something so magical and complete that I would never be the same again."

"Soon I began to fret that my time with Mr. Traveling Man would be far too short, and that I would never be able to harvest all my spiritual needs from his ***Good Book*** before he departed. I had been forever touched by the words within the ***Book***, but I feared that I would be helpless in trying to remember them as I attempted to call them forth from memory once he left. I wished nothing more than to be able to impress the words of **The Good Book** upon my soul forever. But this venerable book was large, and it would take many years to become acquainted with all the words between its pages."

Surprisingly, Selah was an excellent reader. She had always known her gift had been due in part to having a mortal mother bewitched into marrying her father who was a gnome. Her mother had taught her father and herself to read, and she vowed that she would pass this gift along to her infant son as well. Unfortunately, she seldom had the opportunity to use this precious gift since books were scarce and seldom to be seen in the woodlands. She was now ever so thankful that she could now bring this skill to bear upon something so monumental, so earth-shaking; and she now spent hours mesmerized by the pages in the Good Book.

Mr. Traveling Man had graciously invited her into a book that told her how the world began, who her maker was, how the son of the maker became a savior to all who loved and believed in him—promising them a forever life. She had been encouraged to read passages, introduced to the foreignness of new names and prayers upon her tongue, urged to seek answers about how she should live her daily life, and encouraged to initiate a quest for herself—one that she already felt compelled to make.

"Mr. Traveling Man reveals some of life's most important mysteries as he patiently tells me story after story. Though I am truly mesmerized, it is more than that. I feel like I am once again a small child who is being instructed on how to live, and love, and now— grow in faith. My teacher points out specific passages to me from his book, which he also calls **The *Bible*** in a rather hushed tone. I begin to feel my thirsty soul come alive as it is quenched by the *Word of God*. Feelings of joy, and love, and renewal grow within me; and I rejoice that I have not wasted one more day of my life without the knowledge that is being shared with me this day."

Mr. Traveling Man spent five more days visiting Selah and her child in the woodland, and in that precious time he opened her spiritual world in such a way that she knew she would never be the same. She hungered for more and more enlightenment, savoring the glimmer of an eternal spark that had been lit from within, but fearing the day when her visitor would leave her with only the memories of what he had shared with her from his mighty book about God and His Son Jesus.

Selah learned how to pray and how to memorize bits and pieces of ***The Good Book*** that encouraged her transformation. She planned for the day when she would share the teachings from this magical book with her son as he grew in understanding. **The Good Book** acted as an inspiration to her, and she finally decided that she could no longer put off naming her child. His name from this time forward would be Gog—"gift of God." She now knew what blessings were and from whence they came, and she was thankful for that knowledge. Mr. Traveling Man had been sent to her and her child, of that she was convinced, and she owed their precious lives to their Maker.

"On the seventh day of Mr. Traveling Man's stay, he gifted me with my very own **Bible**. My prayers had been answered. No longer would I have to fret about not being able to explore my new faith without **The Good Book** to guide me once he moves on. I won't have to worry about remembering enough and understanding enough to instruct Gog when it comes time to helping him finding his faith. My prayers this night will include how blessed I am for having been gifted with my very own **Bible**. My blessings are many."

Mr. Traveling Man spent much time discussing salvation and baptism with Selah. He showed her where her own name appeared in the pages of **The Good Book**, many times, and yet definition of *Selah* continued to be a mystery—though many somehow felt its importance. They pondered on why some long-ago gnome might have chosen to gift her with this Biblical name. But wasn't so much of life a mystery? Was it realistic to think that all questions came with answers? Selah was a beautiful name, it had come to define who she was, it would last her a lifetime.

When Mr. Traveling Man read to her from **The Good Book**, he brought her closer to God and her savior, Jesus Christ. and she found many Biblical passages to be fascinating, perplexing, and complex; yet she soaked up their imagery like a sponge—for they offered hope for truly connecting with God and His plan for eternal life. It completed something within her spirit, something that had always been lacking.

Finally, on this the very last day of his visit, Mr. Traveling Man took Selah and her child to the banks of the little stream that nestled beyond the cottage so that he could baptize them in its clear water. He pronounced Selah, mother of this child Gog, and Gog, son of his mother Selah, both children of God. He gently pressed his hand down upon each of their heads as he delivered a prayer—giving them into God's care and calling upon Jesus to wash their sins away. He then laid them back in the water for the briefest of immersions—in the name of the Father, the Son, and the Holy Ghost. The day was bright with sunbeams, filled with the serenade of songbirds, and awash with balmy breezes. It was a day of new beginnings for the little family of two. Both had been born again.

Selah prepared a special dinner to celebrate this their day of baptism and to give thanks to Mr. Traveling Man for all he had done for them during his visit. She had begun calling him Mr. Preacher Man shortly after being baptized, revering his skills as a minister and teacher, and knowing that she would never forget him for what he had done for her and her small child. He had become a wonderful spiritual guide and dear friend. His memory would stay with her always. That evening they feasted on partridge eggs, dandelion greens and watercress with vinegar, wild grain flatbreads, and raspberries. They sipped herbal tea sweetened with honey. And after the meal, Mr. Preacher Man taught her the hymn, *Jesus Loves Me.* Selah's heart was full to bursting.

But Preacher Man was not quite through with his lessons. Though he had told Selah many stories: Jesus's birth, his teachings, life with his apostles, his crucifixion on the cross, and his ascension into Heaven to be with his Father—he had never spent much time focusing on communion. He knew in his heart that communion was a very important ceremony because it allowed for continual forgiveness by God and constantly provided hope for eternal life. He could now leave this young mother and her child because he had provided them for a future that included faith.

So, as the shadows began to settle within the cabin, and the embers became reduced to a soft glow, Mr. Preacher Man spread a cloth upon the dining table. He took a bottle of Selah's wild grape wine and a biscuit which he set upon a plate. He retold the moving story of the very first Last Supper that had been hosted by Jesus with his apostles just prior to his crucifixion, and he emphasized both the joy and the sorrow that were to be found at this ceremony that joined heaven and earth: a ceremony that abounded in love and friendship, though tainted by betrayal.

Mr. Preacher Man broke off a piece of the biscuit and told Selah that it was Jesus' body, and then he solemnly ingested it. Then he offered a piece to the mother, and she solemnly chewed and swallowed it. Then he poured a small portion of red wine into a wooden cup and took a small sip, and he told Selah that it was Jesus' blood. And then he offered a sip to Selah. He accompanied his ritual with scripture from **The Good Book** and then led them in a prayer of thanksgiving and promise. This, his last lesson, had been rather solemn, uplifting, poignant, and hopeful. Selah would never forget it.

When Selah awoke the next morning, she took a cup of herbal tea out to Mr. Preacher Man in the hopes of wishing him well before he set out on his journey; but she discovered that he had departed before the break of day. Except for the smallest of blackened coals on the forest floor where his campfire had once been, he had left not a trace.

"I knew deep in my heart that his secretive leave-taking was probably for the best because the week I had spent with him as my guide had been precious beyond belief, and our parting would have been laden with sadness. I wanted nothing to get in the way of the joy that had begun to arise within me, for I would never be the same. I was convinced that he had felt the same way about my conversion to faith. A good shepherd always rejoices when a stray sheep is recovered and returned to the flock. **The Good Book** that Mr. Preacher Man had given me was now propped up on the top shelf of my cupboard in a place of prominence. He had known that becoming a believer was not something that happened overnight, or even over the course of a week. My journey had just begun, and now it would be up to me to explore the many lessons that would guide my life. My heart leapt with love for all that had happened to me with Mr. Preacher Man as my guide, and **The Good Book** represented how my life would be forever changed, and the life of my son's as well."

Mr. Preacher Man's visit had been a pivotal point in my life; and though I never learned who he was, how he had happened to visit me, or who might have sent him—I was content in knowing that it was meant to be. I knew without a doubt that the blessings that he brought to me had been sent from Heaven above."

***

Gog had inherited the faith of his mother. Through her readings and instruction, Selah had taught him valuable lessons in life and spirituality. As his mother, the example that she set was instrumental in fostering his innate goodness and compassion. His life had not always been easy, and he had never expected it to be so. Often throughout the years his life had been filled with trial and tribulation, hardship and pain, and loneliness and sadness. All, however, had been tempered by the beauty of God's world, its bounties that filled many of his human needs, God's words and promises, and the presence of Jesus. And, above all, he was encouraged by the hope for an eternal life that he felt was possible through the grace of God, and because of that he felt rich beyond anything he could imagine.

The elderly gnome now bowed his head in prayer, and his lips gently whispered *The Lord's Prayer*. He felt the Lord's presence, and he trembled. His heart lightened with a gentle sense of forgiveness that flowed to him from above. He knew that he didn't deserve it. Still, he gratefully received it. Another blessing.

Gog stood up and began to retrace the path back to his cottage to begin preparations for his evening meal. His footsteps seemed to be just that much lighter as he walked, his eyes brightly scanning everything along his way in the hopes of discovering something new and marvelous in which to rejoice.

"Spring is filled with so many new beginnings. I even feel changes in my own life. Perhaps because of my faith and the wisdom I seem to sometimes pick up along the way, miraculous change may be possible—even for me, a lowly woodland gnome. I feel that I must take the time to delight in this new world around me, to appreciate its beauty and abundance, and to give thanks to my God in Heaven for it all. Like my friend the garter snake, I feel that I have finally shed my old skin and made way for the new." The gnome began to gently hum a tune as he continued to trudge back to his cottage in the woods.

Chapter 5
World Within A World

Gog had lived many years in his cottage home nestled at the edge of the forest. The cottage was crude but relatively cozy, and what it lacked in beauty it made up for in charm and durability. Almost everything within it was homemade, and most belongings were tinged with age and much use. The home looked lived-in, was not overly-neat, and seemed comfortable like an old shoe. There was always something simmering on the hearth, except perhaps in the very hottest days of summer, and the aroma was quite enough to make your mouth water.

Gog's cottage was truly a world within a world, though he himself was often quite oblivious to those illusive things that were tucked away in secret beneath its eaves. As a woodland gnome who sought the comforts of his home upon crossing its threshold, Gog was often blind to the minutia of everyday existence that filled his living space with a realm of existence beyond his knowledge. Life seemed to pulse in every corner: on the windowsill, in every nook and cranny, and even in the very rafters.

Solomon, the crippled chickadee, was one of the cottage's inhabitants whom Gog knew very well. The tiny bird currently basked in the diluted sun that filtered through the one window, and he cheeped when Gog threw him a few crumbs and a sprinkling of seeds. He cocked his black cap and tipped his head back as he swallowed a drop of water.

Solomon peered out through his bars. *Lonely. I too know loneliness*, thought the little chickadee. *Not a day goes by that I don't regret the fact that I am one of a kind, stranded in a willow cage between my master's cottage walls. I have never forgotten what flying once felt like, what it was to share a nest with siblings, or how much I enjoyed freely foraging for fresh seed and insects. But these memories, though dear, are also quite painful because they are all I have left of my previous life.*

Solomon took a moment to primp, ruffling his feathers and gently rearranging them. He became lost in thought about what had once been. His preening seemed without purpose, though he felt compelled to take a quick bath in his water dish as a stray sunbeam filtered through his cage.

To think that but a few feathers prevent me from joining my flock. The willow bars that enforce the boundaries of my designated home and preserve my safety from outside foes also create my prison. My life has been reduced to slanting rays of sun, crumbs, and droplets. I'm not sure that home and safety are necessarily all that they are cracked up to be. I often think that perhaps the cost is far too high.

Solomon had never questioned Gog's motives for placing him in a cage. He knew with a certainty that his wing had been damaged beyond repair by a collision with an ash tree during a rainstorm. He had accepted the fact that he would never fly again. He also knew that never again would he be able to fend for himself, and that it would have been just a matter of time before he became prey for an owl or a hawk. He also knew that Gog's rationale for his captivity had been pure, based on love and respect for all life.

Above all else, he had wanted to save me, a little bird who had lost its ability to live free! And so—I was saved. Though often I do not always perceive this act of kindness as a true gift, one which should require my thankfulness.

I sometimes wish that I had been allowed to make this final judgment call for myself, thought Solomon. *Freedom and death or imprisonment and life. Perhaps my decision would have been quite the same. Perhaps it would have been quite different. But it would have been my decision, one that I had not been allowed to make on my own.*

I had not been able to share in my own destiny, and that will forever remain a bit of a tragedy.

And so, the tiny chickadee perching upon his twig, continued to offer solace to the lonely gnome and received solace from Gog in return. His early morning *cheeps* greeted the day, and though they were less than enthusiastic, they still contained sweet glimmers of beauty and song. He had a loving soul and made a fine companion, one quite adapted to battling the emotion of loneliness.

Unbeknownst to Gog, Solomon had recently befriended a tiny gray mouse that had scurried through the cottage door one cold and rainy day. The mouse was most certainly a vagrant who, feeling the icy breath of the approaching winter, had decided that a change of scenery might be to his advantage. He had seen that the cottage door had not been closed tightly; and, when he went to explore, he felt the blessed heat that was escaping from within. The mouse was a very young adolescent, quite new to this game of survival; and he had failed miserably in preparing for the cold weather to come: no home, no stored foodstuffs, and separated from a family unable to offer him support and sustenance.

Upon entering the cottage, the little mouse had quickly scurried around its one room looking for an unobtrusive place to call his own. He had thought briefly about his decision to seek shelter within this very strange abode. *I know that I risk much by entering this new world that is so very unlike my own, but my youth and poverty urge me to take the risk. I will never survive long enough to learn life's lessons if I don't do something drastic, something totally immediate, to save myself. The cold weather closes in, and there is nothing anywhere to eat, no warmth and no comfort to be found.*

And so, the little mouse had slipped through a crack in the doorway and immediately become a part of the world within Gog's cottage.

The little mouse was currently invisible to Gog who relied on his sight and hearing to become acquainted with his boarders. The little rodent nested in a discarded old shoe that had fallen behind a stack of firewood. He was soon sharing Solomon's biscuits and dining on the table crumbs that found their way to the rough-hewn wooden floor below. He luxuriated in the heat from the fire upon the hearth and was delighted with his good fortune in finding such a comfortable winter home. He delightedly scampered about the cottage, familiarizing himself with his new address, but remained discreet in his movements. He quietly explored Gog's domain, mostly at night, scavenging as many crumbs and seeds as possible, so that he could munch on them during the day at his leisure and in seclusion.

The mouse had been known as Moon Wink within his own family, but in Gog's cottage he remained nameless. He was an uninvited guest who had arrived unexpectedly, one of a number who often came and went as they pleased throughout the year. After all, he was only boarding for the winter; and the flightless bird was the only one who truly knew of his presence. When spring's balmy winds returned, he would most assuredly make plans to reunite with his family, regain his name, and rejoin the world of the forest glen. For now, though, anonymity was a small price to pay for food and warmth. The mouse occasionally scurried about the house in Gog's absence: visiting Solomon, hoarding crusts of bread, and lining his shoe with more shredded leaves and debris. He felt blessed to find a place where he could eat and sleep in comfort.

The mouse was a merry little presence, but the chickadee couldn't help but envy him his freedom. Their conversations were limited due to their severe language barrier; however, they were able in snippets and bits to amuse and inform each other of the life that went on in this world between cottage walls. Once, the mouse had given Solomon the gift of a dried wild blueberry that had rolled off the table during Gog's meal. Solomon had treasured it for three full days before eating it. Its smell had reminded him of a long-ago summer world of flowers and berries.

The small cottage did have other boarders during these late autumn days. Two ladybug sisters were to be seen from time to time, traversing about on the one forlorn window. Occasionally, they would take wing, but less frequently now that they were becoming sluggish with the cold. They were attracted to what little light remained from behind the windowpanes, and they never made a sound. Sometimes one would be found bottom-up on the sill, having floundered in the window's moisture and rolled over onto her back. When the feeble sun of noon eventually lapped up the dew, the ladybug's shell dried out; and she would right herself and scurry off to another corner of the window.

These occupants were very little company, even to each other, and the mouse and the chickadee proclaimed them rather limited in wit; but they were part of the community. They were of little real interest to the bird and the mouse, for they were not conversationalists, they were very poor listeners, and they certainly appeared dim-witted. Of course, their spotted burnt-orange shells did add splashes of color to this world within cottage walls, especially when they glistened in the sun. And when one lady bug became mired in the dew, again, neither the mouse nor the chickadee could help but be amused.

Three other guests had also gravitated to the window—dark, slender-waisted wasps. The wasps, now they were less than welcome to Solomon and the mouse. These three warlike visitors had invaded their serene space, and they were anything but serene. Their irritating buzz resonated off the cottage walls from sunrise to sunset. Occasionally, the three wasps would ping against the windowpanes as they vainly searched for an escape to the world they saw beyond. They spent much of their time confronting or avoiding each other, for they had no bent for any sort of peaceful co-existence.

The wasps were also seen as rather limited creatures, for in their daily struggles to find an escape route, it never, ever occurred to them that the frigid jaws of Death, borne of an approaching winter, awaited them on the other side of the windowpane. Their actions were based on nothing more than the false dreams of a golden autumn that had long ago come and gone. They droned on and on into space: invading the ladybugs' privacy, pestering the mouse, annoying the chickadee, and continually challenging one another. But they still maintained full use of their wings, and Solomon often took note of this with much envy.

Behind the chimney, in a space no larger than a black walnut, a very small brown bat had also taken up residence so that she could hibernate peacefully over the winter months. There was no room to spare in this nook that provided scant space for her to breathe, but it did possess safety and an opening to the larger world beyond. It was not cold enough for the winter temperatures to erase life, and it was not warm enough to interrupt her winter's slumber. Here she would spend the long months until spring hibernating, waiting for warmer temperatures to thaw her cramped bones. Then she would finally spread her wings for her first flight into the outside world where she would once again seek mosquitoes and other night-flying insects.

Gog, however, was only aware of Solomon, totally oblivious to the existence of the others. When he entered his home at dusk, he sought its shelter, the warmth of the hearth, and the dinner that he would soon set upon the table. By this time all the guests, with the exclusion of Solomon, were silent and hidden in shadow. The only light present came from the leaping flames, slowly simmering the stew and tea, and the stub of a candle on the table that Gog always lit upon his arrival.

One day, Gog brought home another occupant for the cottage—a bedraggled waif, an abandoned late-born kitten, a mewing bundle of matted blonde fur that quickly took to the hearth. Though he had few enough stores for himself and Solomon for the long winter months ahead, the little gnome had been enticed by compassion—for the bobcat kitten's need for a home and his own need for additional companionship. The gnome immediately named the male kitten Daniel, not because he would be thrust into a lion's den but, as a feline member of God's kingdom, he was *of* the lion's den—in a manner of speaking. Half-starved for food, warmth, and most definitely affection—the kitten soon claimed his share of the rustic home. None could even begin to imagine that this innocent-looking furball would soon spell doom for the little mouse who was living a secretive existence, minding his own business, and taking advantage of an opportunity to eke out a living within Gog's cottage. Moon Wink, unfortunately, would never get to reclaim his name or his forest glen.

Gog, though never having realized that a little mouse scurried about his house, had known that adding a bobcat kitten to the cottage would totally change it. "I am so used to being solitary with only my Solomon for company, and though I don't know what I would do without him, there is little enough comfort to be gained from a little lost bundle of feathers in a woven-willow cage. Daniel is a creature who will take food and ease upon my hearth, and I must admit that I look forward to enjoying the warmth of him upon my lap—and perhaps on my pillow at the end of a day. He is another creature to talk to, and his purrs and meows are at the very least the beginnings of conversation. My heart seems to swell a bit as I think about him becoming part of my little family."

Along with the cold that was gradually intensifying day by day, loneliness too had also begun to plague Gog. He could stay busy throughout the day with his chores and explorations; but come evening he would be thrust back to the fireside hearth, which offered physical warmth and comfort but lacked in providing anything to feed a total emptiness of mind and spirit. No other living soul except Solomon met him there to offer companionship and friendship, and often the little chickadee was truly not enough. Hopefully, with the adopted kitten's presence, this aching void might possibly be filled.

The gnome, of course, was a bit oblivious, lacking in foresight regarding the danger that Daniel could impose on some of the smallest creatures within the wooded glen, and even perhaps within his own home. Danger and tragedy could not be so easily recognized when they came in the form of an animal whose claws were sheathed, who gently purred upon the hearth, and who softly padded across the threshold in Gog's wake. The field mouse who slept soundly in his insulated shoe now lived on borrowed time, but he had no reason to believe that he was doomed. In fact, he was totally ignorant of the very concept of Death; and he would never waste his time worrying about something he could only experience but one time.

Daniel had known right away that Gog had provided him with the means to a much better life. In fact, the gnome had quite definitely saved his life.

I cannot believe my luck in having this creature carry me home in his arms. Normally, I would have used my sharp claws to advantage and warned him off by viciously raking them across his arms and legs, throwing in the occasional sharp bite for measure. But with an empty belly and the ice-cold winds burrowing beneath my fur coat, any possibility of finding shelter seemed to me to be an advantage. I remained docile because it seemed the right thing to do in my almost futile attempt at being saved from dire homelessness, and it was probably my very last option for seeking a change in my fortunes.

Of course, upon entering the creature's home, I was immediately drawn to the fire. My body craves the warmth, and I began to tremble as the flames chased away the ice from my blood and the cold from my coat. I could still hear the chill winds whistling at the door, and I felt extremely fortunate in being able to leave them behind. I knew that even my thick fur could no longer totally protect me from them. The aromas coming from the hearth whispered "meat," and I could also smell "bird" and "mouse" in the cottage. When I have had a chance to groom myself and stake out a bed in front of this fire, I will be a new puss indeed.

The kitten rubbed himself against Gog's legs, and his purr echoed throughout the room. Solomon watched the kitten with suspicion; and, though only a bird, he looked at his bars of twig with new respect. His dreams of freedom now took on a much less rosy glow than they had earlier in the day. He fluttered his one good wing to assist him in reaching his perch, and then he settled down with his head nestled beneath it for a bit of a nap.

I know that my sleep will be uninterrupted by any of the other inhabitants, or by the presence of any danger in Gog's cottage. I am a very lucky little bird who has just begun to realize the importance of feeling safe from harm.

Chapter 6
What Is Real?

Gog could not escape his own brotherhood with the life that ebbed and flowed around him. He knew without a doubt that he was but a piece of the puzzle of creation that had been planned by his Maker. Life caught him up in a whirlpool that was dizzying in its power. It led him in a dance that often changed its tempo from slow to fast and fast to slow, a dance that always ended in gentle ripples that lapped at the shore of eternity. It was both a heady experience, and an overwhelming realization, this being part of an awesome master plan. It took much soul-searching and made him take responsibility: to find answers, to discover his purpose, and to take time to count his blessings. He had also discovered that it was by no means a free ride!

Gog often wondered about this thing called existence, "What is real? What can be counted on as being substantial? How do I take my place in this life where reality sometimes battles with myth, and history sometimes jousts with a favorite fairy tale? What can be counted on as being true? What role does my mind play in sorting out what is real?"

Gog thought that if he could see something with his own eyes or touch it with his fingertips that he should be able to count on it as being *real*. He looked closely at his gnarled hand that was covered with callouses. The protruding blue veins pumped lifeblood throughout his body. He flexed his wrist and watched, fascinated, as the sun glinted off the gray hairs that traced his forearm to the elbow. The flexing motion caused his arm muscles to gently ripple. Even in old age he felt strong and filled with this pulsing thing called life. He touched his arm: there was a pulse, it was warm, and though imperfect it worked just fine. It was most definitely substantial—*real.*

The gnome tried to take it one step further. "I am alive, and I experience the world around me; so, therefore, I am real."

"But what of my existence," Gog pondered. "Who in this world knows of it? And isn't my existence tied to what is real? If I were to ask those currently living on earth, would they be able to identify me—a woodland gnome? Would they think of me as being real—or just a figment of their imaginations?"

"I suppose that I could pursue my point even further. Maybe I might examine other creatures recognized in stories and legends. What about a unicorn, as another interesting example? I suppose many might easily believe in the reality of a unicorn without determining the reality of a gnome. Perhaps they are not familiar with my kind. But a unicorn? To me, that seems a bit absurd. Unfortunately, I am convinced that many might be able to draw a rather satisfactory picture of a unicorn, possibly describing it and its habitat, and even discussing the creature's personality. What of a gnome named Gog? Most likely if queried, there would be nothing but silence—silence unbroken by any hint of recognition."

"They might question. 'What is a Gog?' 'Who is Gog?' To all I would be a total unknown. Not a whisper of my *realness* would exist. I do have Solomon, who might vouch for my reality, though he cannot speak. Unfortunately, he would be a very unconvincing witness. Daniel also knows of my existence, but he too is incapable of vouching for me through any sort of common language, especially with the many two-legged beings. My two friends are totally incapable of providing proof of my existence. They cannot prove to anyone in this world that I am *real*."

"God knows of my existence, for it was He who created me. My Savior also knows of my existence, for it is He who is constantly by my side, forgiving my sins and saving my soul. My faith is my very own treasured reality, but I cannot open a chest and display it to anyone. So how do I make it *real* to anyone but myself? Shouldn't things that are so incredibly important be easier to share with the world? I have never *seen* God or my Savior with my own eyes either—though I know without a shadow of a doubt that they are *real.* Whenever I say my prayers, I can sense the presence of God; and I know that He is *real.* But only my own faith can prove this reality, and I'm not sure that my proving the existence of my own faith to others is ever possible."

The poor gnome was boggled by the puzzling concept of what is real, especially as it related to verifying his own existence in the world around him. As a mortal, he felt a bit vulnerable in thinking about his life when comparing it to the existence of so much else in the world. He was certain that this issue was not a priority for others, so he wondered if he might just be spinning his wheels as he thought about the concept of *what is real.*

"Is *real* really real?" Gog puzzled. "Or is reality just a puzzle that is lacking a solution? The unicorn in this situation has the upper hand, of that I am sure. Many more know of him than of me—though he is but a myth."

The gnome sighed. "Even though I can feel my own arm, experience its power, and acknowledge it as one of my limbs—I am but a sole witness. I look in the mirror and peer into my own sad brown eyes, recognizing a lonely soul with whom I have kept company for a great many years. The unicorn is just some fancy of the Universe that has galloped into the imagination of those hungry for fantasy and myth. Yet, it has continued to exist in the minds of millions for centuries. My life, to most all on this earth, is in truth close to being invisible; for it has never been seen nor understood to exist. It's as if I had never been brought to life, though I myself know that my life is my most precious possession. I'm convinced that I will never reach a conclusion about this most puzzling state of being!"

The confusion created about what is *real* and what is not was both fascinating and troubling to the gnome. In all his days he would never be able to reconcile himself as to how to proceed with his viewpoint about his own existence.

"But who is *more* real? The unicorn or me?" Gog puzzled. His answer varied from day to day.

***

Existence is an awesome concept, a blending of sweet joy and horrific sorrow that makes life both interesting and challenging. Sometimes existence for Gog was extremely painful, especially following the death of his mother. To escape the pain of his grief and loneliness, he sometimes envisioned himself soaring out of his physical self, which at times had become a prison—a place where he was forced to deal with his losses. He sometimes sought to find a way to free himself from the cares of the world, feeling compelled to move Heaven and earth to escape the sadness found within.

One day, during one of these moods, Gog strolled to the very edge of a towering, jagged cliff. He peered down into the valley below where the grasses and bushes appeared to be a silvery green. Swirls of mist seemed to scale the steep sides of the cavern that was found within. The floating mist that enveloped the descent with a certain dreaminess held the gnome spellbound.

Gog heard cries that echoed throughout the valley and, when he looked up above himself and into the sky, he caught sight of a pair of eagles. He marveled at them as they glided effortlessly on the invisible air currents with such freedom and majesty that they appeared to float with virtually no earthly ties.

"When I think about my own existence, I wonder how I might be able to escape my present misery. Sometimes it is hard to feel joy when the sadness presses down upon me. If I could only free myself from my pain like the eagles do with their miraculous flights that cut their bonds with gravity how much happier I would be. How do I rid myself of the sadness that subdues my natural good spirits? How do I break free from the evil forces that often persuade me to focus on the darkness in my life?"

As Gog looked down into the valley below, he thought of nothingness—of a total loss of existence and memory that just might erase all his pain. Oblivion beckoned him. Somehow, totally losing himself by plunging into total nothingness seemed to be a most positive proposition. "I could escape all of my earthly troubles. I would delight in freeing myself from all pain and responsibility. In one moment, I could ease the pain and sorrow that lingered in my heart."

He continued to watch the eagles in their miraculous flight, and he thought about this new kind of freedom that might forever release him from all the sadness and loneliness that currently enveloped him.

"I could effortlessly soar like the eagles. For a short while I could leave all my sorrows behind. I could decree my own freedom and pursue my own destiny without being accountable to anyone but myself. I could escape all of my woes."

Then Gog began to frown as he struggled with the responsibility of making a choice that he was forcing upon himself—the choice to leave his own world behind him without respectful acknowledgment of God and Jesus. "Is it right that I choose to leave all I know and love behind me because I long for a glimpse of the total freedom that might be mine to keep if I were to leave this world? Would this become an act of self-completion or pure selfishness? Freedom or annihilation? Have I not been privy to many divine lessons from Above that have offered me love, forgiveness, and strength? I am but one lost soul, however, and am I not truly worth my Maker's concern?"

"I do so thirst for something that will immediately ease my loneliness and my pain. And I most definitely continue to wonder what the feeling of total freedom might be like. I think I know. It would be wonderful! I can just imagine the breath of the wind supporting my limbs while I float gracefully for the first few seconds until my plummet is met by the rush of acceleration and my body quickly picks up momentum and drops like a rock into the great unknown. The rush of wind! The speed of my falling body! The final plummet. . ."

Gog sharply inhaled as his imagination tempted fate. He knew that he was considering an attempt at changing the course of his life on a mere whim, and yet—it was most certainly enticing. He somehow felt that there was a Darkness tempting his soul to decisively choose something that was both liberating and easy. Unfortunately, this decision also seemed somehow to be linked to Evil and destructive forces. He rapidly blinked and wondered further about the magnitude of his decision.

"The plummet would be both scary and exhilarating. But it would be final. All decision-making would be torn from me forever. There would be no going back. My existence would no longer be. The gnome Gog would immediately cease to exist. In one brief moment, I would toss my life away on a very powerful but selfish whim."

The wind elicited a muted wail, and a chill raced up and down the gnome's spine. He shivered at the magnitude of his imaginings.

"I do not wish to think beyond the final exhilarating leap. I cannot. The leap would be exciting. What would come next—would not. Though I do not wish to think before I act, I know that I must. This deed that I contemplate is far more than crossing a bridge; it's a temptation that is calling upon me to ignore my faith in God. I absolutely cannot think of this world without myself in it; and, somehow, it strikes a definite feeling of horror within me. I am the only main character in my story of life that has any real believability to me. A tale without me would be no tale at all."

Gog understood why he was drawn to this temptation. It seemed that the pain he experienced had continued to exist in some form or another for far too long. Perhaps he had spent too much time in thought: reminiscing, pondering his choices, chasing some very unrealistic dreams. Now it seemed he just wanted to simply stop thinking! "Thinking has certainly never given me much peace of mind."

As the gnome teetered on the very edge of the precipice, looking down into the soft green canyon below, he began to imagine a kind of perfect peace—a peace that made him feel the lightness of nothingness. It was a seductive moment. He longed for this sense of peace with all his heart. But he knew without a doubt that there would be ramifications, so he refused to continue exploring them.

"All the pain I face daily could be immediately erased: loneliness, worry, disenchantment, and sadness. The burden of old age. All gone!" He looked with longing at the misty grasslands below that beckoned, ready to embrace him. He spread his arms and swayed above the abyss, and the wind ruffled his hair. He began praying for the kind of peace that was far beyond his understanding.

Gog's prayer was quickly answered by a convulsion of conscience. He immediately realized that his prayer had not been about seeking guidance from above but soliciting confirmation for his selfish plans to do away with himself—forever. He quickly took a step back from the lip of the cliff. "Totally leaving this world and all I know? Forever? For me to be no more— through my own choice. Immediately forgotten by the few who know me. What of their dependence upon me? Forgotten by all. To become nothing. Immediately and with no going back." He choked in horror!

"What of my responsibility to my mother's spirit which is imprisoned in my bottle? What of my plans for our future journey to heaven together, and my hope for my own redemption? Would my freedom be worth leaving my mother suspended in limbo until God sets her free one day? Would sacrificing my own life be worth the risk of condemning my own soul for eternity, of imprisoning it in a hell of its own making because I am intent on erasing my pain—so much borne of my own selfishness?"

Gog brought himself up short and stood erect as he chastised himself, "I haven't the right! It would be like destroying a gift in front of the giver. I have a Maker who loves me, and He is responsible for my existence. He created me; and upon my own timely death, He will welcome me home My life is precious! It is nothing that should be tampered with on a whim."

"Haven't I blessings aplenty? Hasn't the good Lord seen fit to care for me with food, shelter, and the glories of nature?" Gog bowed his head. He quickly backed away from the precipice in shame, slowly shaking his head in self-disgust.

Gog thought about this personal quest which might have erased all pain and sorrow. "Am I truly seeking peace? Or is it Death I seek, the finality of all that I am or ever could be? Each life is truly a miracle. How could self-destruction ever be considered a means to gaining peace?"

The gnome knew that he had only been fooling himself. He had allowed an unholy niche to open wide within his soul to invite Darkness and repel *The Light*. He needed, instead, to seek an inner peace that was somehow connected to his Maker. His focus should be on the creation of possibilities for his life, not on his own destruction! He should never give evil the opportunity to suggest his own life's path, for its deceitful ways invariably led to the annihilation of life, love, and faith.

The gnome became less confused the further he walked away from the cliff. In his mind's eye his existence took on the vibrant colors of one who chose life whole-heartedly, one who constantly continued to strive for goodness through God. Gog was a modest version of man, an inhabitant of the Hinterland, a member of a proud race whose time was now short. He was solitary—the last remaining woodland gnome still holding out for all eternity. He was also God's creation.

"Yet, though I deeply feel the bitterness of regret as it assaults me with the reminder of what I almost chose as my fate, I realize that I should have never allowed the Darkness of my soul the opportunity to seek such a selfish triumph. It would have destroyed my Light, and I would have been forever lost."

As creatures went, Gog was luckier than most. He had reaped years and years of a rather golden harvest: he had been loved, fed, and raised in faith. He had received blessings a-many and known much contentment. He was of the fortunate. Straightening his hat, he stuck his hands in his pockets and shuffled back to his cottage where he knew that he would be welcomed home. The eagles' eerie cries could still be heard in the distance, but Gog did not look back.

***

Gog was fortunate that his slumbers were most frequently of a peaceful nature. Before bed, he took the time to settle his mind from the day's trials and tribulations with prayer and a thanksgiving of his blessings. Covered in a quilt soft with age where his large tawny tomcat nestled firmly against him, his dreams were imaginative visions of what had been and what might come. His snores rumbled from deep within his chest, often noisily escaping his mouth with a whistle or a gasp. Sometimes Daniel gently laid a paw upon Gog's lips, attempting to restrain his keeper from making so much noise. He did not enjoy having his own sleep interrupted.

It was in the waking hours before dawn when Gog's soul arose and flew to the neighboring souls where it paused, surveyed, and then returned to Gog— satisfied in some ways and left wanting in others. Its gossamer wings beat greedily upon the moisture-laden air, searching for a heavenly current that would thrust it spiraling for another exhilarating joyride.

When fully awake the next morning, Gog lay there and pondered his dream state the night before, wondering if the journey had been a figment of his imagination or a glimmer of heavenly truth. “I wonder if these travels are in vain or if they are sent to assist me on my own life’s journey. Are these dream journeys of my slumber real? Do they need only exploration and interpretation so that they may guide me through this life? Or are they phantoms borne of my imagination that exist only to entertain me in my sleep state?”

The clock in the entryway could be heard, “tick-tock, tick-tock, tick-tock.” The hour chimed, and Gog quickly arose to don his overalls. The sun, illuminating the dew on the grass by his doorstep, greeted him; and he greedily inhaled the night-cooled air that surrounded his clearing. Daniel joined him upon the stoop, rubbing his furry back against Gog’s legs. The gnome petted his cat, fetched a bucket of cold spring water, and then went back inside the cottage to cook his breakfast. Another day. He gave thanks.

Gog heard his stomach growl. He felt hunger pains. And they were very real!

Chapter 7
A Cottage Garden

Gog often viewed life as a mystery of fantastic proportions, and nothing was an example of this mystery any more than the cottage garden that he planted every spring. He tilled the rich earth by hand— earth fragrant with leaf mold, compost, and wood ash. His rows were often crooked and sometimes oddly spaced. The seeds that he planted, dried and preserved from the summer harvest before, were always vital and seemingly anxious to transform themselves into green.

The gnome believed that all this new life that took root in his cottage garden was based on miracle upon miracle. The dried husks of seed that were sown by his own hand contained that tiny but mighty spark of life that had been held hostage until man or nature set it free to become a seedling by merging it with soil, moisture, and sunshine.Gog was always mesmerized by the miraculous change that always took place. "First, I marvel at the escape of the seedling from its husk. When the tiny spark within the seed swells in triumph to such an extent that it finally bursts its ties and immediately sends out roots, stems, and leaves, I feel a real sense of exhilaration."

"Even the tiniest of seeds holds the knowledge of its destiny within its tiny frame, so a carrot seed always becomes a carrot and a pumpkin seed always becomes a pumpkin.

Little seeds, seeds no bigger than a tick, and large seeds, sometimes as big as buttons, it makes no difference— all are programmed by the Maker to create new plants with *blueprints* that lie deep within them. This new life almost never strays from the glory of its identity. It is utterly amazing!"

Gog always planted his garden just after dawn on a bright sunny morning, after the soil had been kissed by the warmth of the sun's rays and dampened by numerous nightly dews and spring showers. It seemed that almost overnight the rows became brilliant lines of varying shades of green. The garden quickly began to grow, encouraged by the soil's fertility, the gentle spring rains, and Gog's persistent care.

If the growing season remained successful, the seedlings would quickly grow thick and tall; and they would rapidly begin competing for space. They always seemed anxious to make their way in the world: hungry for the soil's nutrients, thirsty for the rain, and greedy for the sun's rays. But as they grew, the tiny garden patch seemed to, almost immediately, dwindle in size as the robust plants pushed against the order of their rows and, sometimes, against each other.

Gog stood by his garden with his gnarled hands on his hips and frowned. "Now comes the part that I dread with a passion—the thinning of the seedlings, deciding which ones will live and which ones will be plucked to die. I will be the one responsible for making the judgment call on each plant that falls under my scrutiny."

From the triumphant emerging of the seedlings from the fertile soil, it now became more and more evident that all that grew side by side could not possibly share in the destiny of life. For some seedlings to inherit their birthright as mature plants, others must be thinned out and left in the space between the rows to perish. The gnome slowly worked each row somberly, trying to apply a method of reasoning to each decision in plucking random seedlings out of his garden to provide those that remained with the space that they would need to grow. His decisions were never easy.

"Usually I leave the strongest, the thickest, the healthiest; but sometimes I can't help myself, and on the rare occasion I find that I might pull a large and healthy seedling in deference to its smaller, more fragile, neighbor—just because I want to give the weaker seedling a chance to prove itself, now that it is no longer bullied by crowding neighbors who rob it of sunshine and moisture."

"Sometimes I am rewarded for my decision. The seedling grows tall and strong and matures into a wonderful vegetable for harvest. But sometimes the weaker seedling gradually withers and dies—seemingly for no reason. It lacks vitality and fails to thrive even when given the opportunity. Its brief existence is marked only by the empty space in the row where the other seedlings continue to flourish and prosper. Often, neighboring seedlings take the opportunity to thrust themselves into the vacancy in the row so that their roots, stems, and leaves prosper to a far greater extent because of this unexpected gift of additional space. Thinning my seedlings can sometimes be a most sad proposition altogether."

Gog also transplanted seedlings from his lean-to, seedlings that he had carefully sown earlier, weeks before he had planted his actual garden. The plants had started their existence in a protective nook that was covered by sheltering branches in the evening until the last threats of frost had passed. The nook, which in some ways resembled a nursery, had been banked by rich compost to hold frost at bay. Its southern exposure had provided the numerous tender seedlings with much-needed sunshine and heat at the very break of day.

These favored seedlings had led very sheltered lives and consisted mostly of tomatoes, peppers, and an assortment of herbs—plants that craved the sun and its heat and were extremely susceptible to the cold. The growing of tomatoes and peppers could not be rushed, for these vegetables required a rather lengthy season to mature. The herbs seemed always eager to flourish in whatever space was allotted to them. When these seedlings leafed out, outgrowing their manmade nursery, Gog carefully transplanted them to their section of the garden where they could take full advantage of the elements and where they would not be shaded. Here they would prosper until some needed to be staked; and all needed to be fed additional nutrients from the compost bin, mulched with forest leaves, and generously watered.

The garden always boasted an outside row of spinach, loose-leaf lettuce, and spring onions. They did not mind a bit of shade; and, in fact, it sometimes prevented them from prematurely "bolting" and going to seed. A few maples stood to their side, blocking some of the very most direct sun. This row of greens decorated the entry to the garden, adorning its perimeter like an emerald necklace. These would be the first garden vegetables to mature, and Gog always looked forward to this early harvest. He would bring them to his table with delight, savoring the flavor and freshness of his very first vegetables of the year's harvest. Though by this point, the gnome had already feasted on dandelion greens, cowslip greens, and fiddleheads from the wild—the addition of lettuce and onions for his salad and spinach for his soup pot or cooked to be eaten with vinegar were always welcome additions to his daily menu.

The garden plot was the lifeblood of Gog's little homestead. Its benefits were immeasurable to him in so many ways. As he journeyed along the path to access it, he was so often reminded of the benefits and wonders of spring.

"The hard work in the open air always strengthens my body after a long winter of relative inactivity. The warm sun and soft breezes encourage my mind to wander in pleasant thought. The fresh air is stimulating, and as I wander through my woodlands I constantly make new discoveries each and every day: the frog eggs in the swamp that will soon turn into pollywogs, the orange newts that cover my pathway to my garden after an evening rain, the half-grown squirrels that chase their brothers and sisters around and around the tree trunks, and the hatch of wood ducklings that quietly follow their mother into the shallows of the gurgling brook."

"I love the natural world, but my garden is my greatest treasure. When I work it, I feel happiness, hope, and prosperity. The fresh vegetables provide my body with necessary nutrition, and they act as a wonderful spring tonic so that I feel stronger and have more energy. If I am blessed with good weather, and my health is such that I can maintain my garden as well as harvest it, it will take me throughout the entire year with fresh, stored, canned, pickled, and dried vegetables. It will feed my body, my mind, and my soul. I will be its more-than-willing servant while it grows and matures because its benefits will far outweigh any of the labor that it will receive from my hand."

As each season progressed, Gog stood guard over his little garden. He pulled the weeds that competed with the vegetables and herbs for moisture and nutrients, plucked harmful insects from the leaves and stalks, provided the ground with water from his well when rain was scarce; and scattered buckets of fallen leaves between the rows to provide a path, retain moisture, and choke out the marauding weeds that were constantly sprouting. The late spring and early summer months were busy months, for the success of the gnome's vegetable garden was a must if he was going to successfully survive the cold winter that always loomed just beyond the next harvest.

"It seems that my garden is always quick to reward me for my labors. The garden greens and the spring onions always lead the parade of edibles to be harvested, and they are soon followed by peas, cucumbers, beet greens, new potatoes, and tomatoes. As summer begins to come to an end, I will glean the last of the early harvest and tend to my winter vegetables that will eventually be stored before the hard frost: pumpkins, beets, squash, turnips, parsnips, potatoes, and cabbage."

Gog was seldom disappointed by the bounty of his garden. And if for some reason his garden failed by becoming stunted or damaged by a cool, damp summer, a blistering drought, or an extremely early frost, enough so that his supply of vegetables was less than expected; he would just do the very best he could do given the situation. He would spend more time gleaning foodstuffs from the neighboring meadows and woodlands, attempting to make up for the shortage. Mushrooms, berries, nuts, and wild grains would be found and harvested—especially in much larger quantities than usual.

The gnome had been very fortunate over the years, for he had never been forced to live through a winter in total want. And his garden had to take most of the credit for this.

Gog sometimes stood leaning on his hoe, contemplating his cottage garden that provided him with so many herbs and vegetables. He felt surrounded by a magical world of plenty. "I sometimes see my garden as my very own kingdom with myself as its ruler. As its king, my royal subjects are many: the new seedlings and the mature plants; the brightly colored vegetables and herbs; and the flowers. They totally rely on me, the soil beneath their feet, moisture, and the weather. I take my vows as their king seriously, making sure that all my subjects in the garden are guarded, protected, and nurtured. It is a joyful burden that I carry until the day of harvest."

The gnome knew that a king alone could not take full responsibility for the success of the garden. Gog always did what he could do within his own capacity as the gardener. In any kingdom there must also be knights and retainers available to assist their king in the call of duty. Gog was not shy about giving credit where credit was due. He looked about his kingdom of the cottage garden and recognized that there were many workers who were constantly mobilizing for his cause.

"My kingdom includes a royal army, as all kingdoms must, to patrol and assist its monarch. This loyal army includes honeybees, butterflies, and wasps that pollenate it; praying mantises, lady bugs, and toads that do battle with those insects that would ravage it; and snakes, owls, foxes, and hawks that are vigilant in hunting the rodents that are intent upon destroying its harvest. Without my army, my garden would constantly be far more vulnerable to attack. I am very grateful to all those in my kingdom who take up the gardening crusade year after year. My little kingdom is truly a miracle to behold!"

"You might say that I am rather an unusual king in that I enjoy spending my time in my garden hoeing the soil, watering the plants, and mulching between the rows of vegetables. I know that these tasks have much to do with physical labor, but they are completely necessary in helping to insure my garden's success. Never a day goes by that I don't give a word of thanks to my faithful royal army. When it comes time for the harvest, I am always humbled by the quality and quantity of vegetables that I'm able to store in my cottage for the winter months—true treasure from my garden for my kingdom, for those who depend upon it for their very lives. I also never forget for a moment from whence comes the true blessings of my precious garden's bounty—from the good Lord above. I give thanks."

Chapter 8
Putting By Sustenance

Though Gog's freedom from hunger truly began in his cottage garden, a large part of its bounty was held fast and secure within the dark, gloomy cavern of his root cellar in preparation for the winter months ahead. After many years of hardship with their food supply, he and his mother had realized that they needed a storage area that could maintain a consistent, cool temperature, though not freezing, where they could store their yearly harvest. Previously, most of their vegetables had been tied to the rafters in the cottage where they were gradually dried and smoked by the fire. This was not very effective because the dried produce was never very tasty, and much of it eventually spoiled.

Finally, a much younger Gog had labored for many weeks to construct a winter storage area beneath the cottage floor. He had excavated a very large hole by chiseling shovelful after shovelful of clay, loam, and rocks from beneath their home. He had removed the excess dirt one bucket at a time, forming a pile as a natural barrier to the back of his garden. He had propped up the cottage floor with cedar timbers, and rock columns were strategically laid at each corner of the cellar so that the underground room under construction would not cave in upon him while he worked and would provide solid support to the structure after its completion. These columns would also give additional strength to the cottage floor above this new storage space.

Once the ceiling support for the root cellar was complete, Gog had lined the room's walls with large rocks that were then covered by crudely-planed cedar shakes.

Thick shelves and bins were crafted from thin slabs of slate that were supported by rock supports. A sturdy three-board cedar door was attached with hinges that had once been attached to the lid of an old trunk that had finally succumbed to an infestation of wood beetles. By the end of that summer, the root cellar had been made ready to receive the upcoming fall harvest—for the very first time.

The root cellar's ceiling was barely five and a half feet high. Even Gog had to stoop a bit in places whenever he ventured below for a potato, a jar of tomatoes, or a turnip. The space was insulated enough with rock, slate, and clay to maintain a much cooler environment during the warmer months while it was insulated enough to protect the stored vegetables and fruits from the deepest of winter freezes.

This harvest den was dark and dank. Water dripped from the stone-lined walls, and the cold and damp could sometimes numb limbs. Occasional gusts of wind moaned around a few of the chinks in the walls, and the drip. . .drip. . .drip from ground water was hypnotic. The cellar, though reminding him of nothing less than a burial tomb which spoke of death and decay because of its cold, dark atmosphere, was filled with life-sustaining food for the duration of the long winter months.

Gog often shook his head in bewilderment due to the mixed emotions he often felt upon visiting this latest addition to their home, "When I visit the root cellar to retrieve some of the stored goods, I am always of two minds. I feel so secure and blessed to have this wide array of food at my fingertips for my very survival, for I know that there are many creatures who live through much of the winter with empty bellies. I know that to be able to live without hunger is a wonderful blessing. Unfortunately, my cellar also speaks of the Darkness found in some souls—and Death. The cold, dank atmosphere—important for preserving foodstuffs—also feeds the imagination with a sense of doom and desolation."

"My first response to all my visits always begins positive. To think that just a few months ago this treasure trove had been gathered from my very own garden makes me incredibly proud, and I feel a wonderful sense of accomplishment. I must say that my stored vegetables do provide a splendid sight, and they alone make me smile."

"The feeble, flickering of my candle rests upon sodden slate shelves that exhibit rows of jars—jars that glimmer with the gemlike light of summer as they sit in their dusty glory: ruby tomatoes, golden corn, amethyst beets, and emerald beans. In soggy wooden bins potatoes, turnips, carrots, wild apples, and cabbages are stored. In the spring the potatoes will send forth anemic shoots that appear to be attempting a bold escape from their dungeon. The carrot, turnip, and cabbage bins will most often be empty by then, and the remaining apples—pungent with rot and mold."

"As my eyes become accustomed to the lack of light, and the cold begins to seep into my bones, I cannot help but feel overwhelmed by a dark mood that always tends to come over me in this space. It is impossible not to compare these surroundings with a grave, and the specter of Death always seems to intrude. Though I try with all my might not to let these dark feelings conquer me, it is almost impossible. I must continually remind myself that when spring comes along again, I will plant numerous seed potatoes in my rich garden soil; and their healthy sprouts will bring forth a new crop. My empty jars will be purified with boiling water from my cauldron and refilled with more colorful fruits and vegetables. And gentle breezes and the light of day will eventually scour this den clean, preparing it for yet another harvest. For now, I shiver and wrap my arms closely around my body as I search for a jar of preserves."

Not much ever ventures into this subterranean world, though a few hardy salamanders have called it home, and a few reclusive spiders have sometimes spent days draping it with web. In the spring box turtles have been known to wander in when the door was opened to cleanse the cellar with fresh air and light. But for the most part, the root cellar constantly exhibits a most bleak and unwelcoming environment.

Gog himself never stayed below longer than was necessary. Though the loaded shelves and full bins spoke of harvest plenty, and he felt a sense of well-being because all his stores were safely tucked aside for winter, these visits only heightened his sense of loneliness. Here he was pointedly reminded of his own fragile mortality. The cellar's tomblike atmosphere was claustrophobic and reeked of Death and decay.

"I know that my root cellar is indeed a Godsend, yet I cannot help but believe that in the depths of winter, along with vegetables and fruits, there is a presence that resides there as well—and this presence is dark, fearsome, and does not wish me well."

***

Once spring surrounded the little cottage, Gog began his daily tramps into the woodlands, along the creek, and through the fields. Though he was able to grow and preserve much of his own food, he knew that it was important to gather what he could from nature as well. The foods he gathered from his tramps included foods that he would immediately eat fresh that very day or would store for a day when there was a scarcity.

The foods that Gog gathered and ate fresh were important because they allowed him to preserve and store more of what his garden produced. He took advantage of the woodland's fiddleheads, the creek's watercress, the swamp's marsh marigold greens, and the meadow's dandelion greens—all eaten fresh, some with vinegar. He pilfered a few fresh eggs in the early spring from the nests of turkeys, geese, ducks, and partridge—never taking more than an occasional egg from any nest.

Gog was fortunate in that he could also gather many foodstuffs directly from nature to supplement his wintertime larder. He gathered wild grains from the grasses in the field and acorns and walnuts from the trees in the woodland. He would later grind some of them to make flour. He also picked wild apples for cider and vinegar, to be stored fresh in his root cellar, and to be strung and dried in his rafters.

Honey made from the wildflowers of the meadow was one of the most important foodstuffs that Gog sought in his woodlands. The honey, along with a few bricks of maple sugar, were his only sweeteners, and both were highly prized for his baking and in making preserves.

Gog constantly searched for honey sources on many of his expeditions. He had become adept at following the honeybees from locations where they had been gathering pollen from various blossoms back to their hive, most often found in the hollow of a tree. He would smoke the bees out with a smoldering rag, and their state of drowsiness allowed him to take a bit of their honeycomb filled with honey, without being stung. The bees would immediately go back to making more honey, and soon honey would drip from their hive once more. Never did Gog take any of the bee's honey after summer began to wind down into fall, for the bees would need these stores for themselves to guarantee their own survival over the long winter months. He would also render the beeswax gathered, turning it into candles to light his cottage when winter's deep shadows fell.

Gog was also adept at making maple bricks for his winter larder. At the end of March, he drilled holes in a few of the sugar maple trees in his woods and tapped them with hand-whittled wooden spigots. The sap from these trees would slowly drip when the weather became warm enough, and it was slowly collected in the wooden buckets that he hung below the spigots. Then he would collect the sap and pour it into his cauldron over the fire in his summer kitchen, cooking it slowly over a low heat. As the sap bubbled away, the air would fill with plumes of steam and sweetness. When it boiled down to such a point that it was beginning to crystallize into sugar, the gnome would watch it very carefully until it lost most of its moisture and was ready to be pressed into molds to make the maple bricks.

"I know that I may go to a lot of trouble in providing sweetness for my household. I must admit that I alone have a bit of a fondness for sweets and, though I also enjoy the sweetness of the many woodland fruits and berries, these sweeteners from the bee and the maple that I crave are always welcomed—for my porridge, tea, and baked goods. And, of course, the honey and maple sugar serve a very practical purpose as well; for they are useful in preserving my jams and canned fruits, and in making wine for the winter. The winter months are long, and many a dark, lonely night is made pleasurable while I sit beside my fire with the sweet earthly delights of a baked apple, a cup of hot tea, or a mug of wild grape wine."

Gog always collected a wide variety of special herbs like mint, nettles, sassafras, comfrey, and certain wildflowers; as well as an assortment of tree bark taken from the willow, the sumac, the maple, and the birch. All these were dried for use as teas and remedies. He collected sacks of mushrooms and fungi and baskets of wild grapes, blueberries, blackberries, and raspberries. If foodstuffs seemed scarce on any given day, he would turn to filling his haversack with kindling wood, something of which he could never have too much. He would stack it by the backdoor of his cottage in front of his very large woodpile. Gog was most definitely hard-working, but it was of necessity.

Many of the various foodstuffs, were stored in the cottage itself. The rafters held ropes of onions and garlic, bunches of herbs and wild grains, garlands of dried apples and berries, and strings of mushrooms and wild flowers. Fruits would be dried or pressed into juice for wine, tonics, or vinegar. All would be put to beneficial use. During the winter months Gog lived on a wide variety of soups, stews, and pungent teas; and for an entire year these herbs and seasonings were sparingly used to season his meals and to provide their many healing properties in broth or health-giving concoctions.

Hunting and gathering everything necessary to keep his body and soul together was a lot of work, but Gog treated it all as both a blessing and a challenge. He felt secure in knowing that somehow through his diligence and God's goodness that he would be provided for, and that the challenge it provided him as he secured these needs kept his wits alive, fulfilled his questing nature, and humored his thirst for knowledge. Seeking his cottage at the end of the day, with his knapsack bulging with nature's treasures, was a great reward; and he humbly rejoiced in the work of the day.

Gog waited out each evening in late fall, winter, and early spring by huddling near the crackling fire on the hearth while his meal simmered in the kettle. The cold, wild winds frequently buffeted his snug little home, attempting to bully their way in through the chinks, down the chimney, and around the window frame. Gog would twiddle his thumbs, read by candlelight, or sip on cups of hot, mulled wine from a few dusty bottles of honey-fermented wild grape and dandelion wines. The hot wine would warm that part of his body that could not be warmed by soup or tea alone, and it would leave him drowsy and ready for his long winter's nap.

"I often sit in the old oak rocking chair which has a very long history unknown to anyone now living. I swaddle myself in my mother's thick but shabby woolen shawl; and I think about her, enjoying its comfortable warmth as it surrounds me. I watch the firelight flicker and dance upon the blackened chimney wall, and I relax and feel blessed that my cottage keeps winter's icy breath away from my door. I close my eyes and proceed to dream of the gentle sun and mild breezes of a distant spring morning, and I imagine the chirp of an early robin."

"I find contentment in my home, for isn't my belly filled with food, my body warmed by fire and drink, and my head filled with dreams and memories? My larder is filled with sustenance for the long winter ahead guaranteeing that my body will easily survive winter's deprivation. Now my mind begins to quietly gather its thoughts and ideas so that soon it will be brimming with the memories of my long life's journey, sustenance for my brain's long winter of remembering and imagining."

Chapter 9
Mr. Fellows' Visit

On the back of Gog's cottage, a crude but solid lean-to had been constructed, a summer kitchen of sorts. Nestled as it was against the chimney, the space retained enough warmth so that in winter things seldom froze here, but the temperatures were cool enough here in summer to protect those items that needed to be guarded against too much heat. This lean-to was used as a pantry for storage, a kitchen where Gog could cook over a small open fire without overheating his cottage during the summer months, and a garden shed. Here he stored his gardening tools and some of his stores of food in crocks and jars.

It was in the pantry section that wine and sauerkraut were fermented and then stored in crocks. Maple sugar was stored in cakes, combs of honey were arranged in a metal box, and jugs of wild apple vinegar were corked and kept in a food safe. Dried beans and the seeds for spring planting were also kept here, safe in their glass jars with sturdy lids.

One day, when Gog ventured into the pantry for a jug of wine with which to warm himself on an especially brutal January evening, the glow of his candle caught a flicker of movement. At first, he was startled, but then he saw that his light held a pair of piercing black eyes hostage in its rays. A small field mouse in its brown velvet tuxedo with white weskit stared back at him, fear evident in his stare. At first Gog looked around for a weapon with which to dispose of the unwanted intruder, but something held him back.

"My mind tells me this mouse may very well become a pest, but all the foodstuffs in my pantry are well-protected. I know that the little mouse is here due to the cold and deprivation. My heart can't help but go out to him." Gog watched with interest as the mouse scurried away, disappearing into the gloom beyond the candle's glow.

The mouse took on very different proportions that day. From being first portrayed as an unwanted intruder, he soon was acknowledged as a cherished guest—a long-lost relative who had come to spend the winter months. Gog was intrigued.

"Mr. Fellows shall be my new friend's name, and I will certainly pray that the mouse is a "he," as I first guessed, and is not weighed down by unborn offspring. I must see to his needs and make sure that he is provided with a decent meal. I'm sure that he is an enterprising little fellow and that he will make his own way in setting up a home."

Every evening Gog began leaving a little saucer of tidbits for Mr. Fellows: dried beans, biscuit crumbs, a few sunflower seeds, chunks of carrot, a fleshy apple core. All would be gone in the morning. Gog eventually discovered the mouse's winter home, an empty jar hidden behind a large crock that he had ingeniously filled with the shredded burlap from a discarded, rotting sack. Gog was impressed at the diligence and ingenuity that had created the comfortable mouse house. He knew that Mr. Fellows would be snug and warm there for the duration of the winter months.

Gog caught glimpses of his new friend from time to time. Most were fleeting. A few times they were not. Mr. Fellows was really a very handsome little mouse. Gog continued to hope he was a *fellow* and not a pregnant female. He could tolerate one guest, but he knew that he did not want to be over-run by mice by spring. A month passed, and he breathed a sigh of relief; his guest remained solitary, and the scampering that he occasionally heard came solely from him.

The gnome found himself visiting the pantry far more frequently than he had ever visited it in the past. Each day he vied with the previous day in leaving the choicest of tidbits for his little houseguest: stale biscuit, dried apple slices, a few parched kernels of corn, a dried blackberry; and each day he smiled with pleasure when he viewed the empty plate from which his friend had dined. There was great comfort to be found in taking care of one of the Maker's creatures, even—or more especially—if he was but a humble field mouse, dressed in his velvety best to be sure.

As time went by, Mr. Fellows became less cautious when he heard Gog's approach. He was a personable little mouse, and his little whiskers twitched with curiosity when the gnome replenished his saucer, wondering what the offering of the day might be. He sometimes wondered what kind of creature would set out such a fine dinner without a by-your-leave, and he would watch his waiter very carefully when he set down the plate to see if there might be an ulterior motive. There never was, however, and the little mouse soon began to feel comfortable in Gog's presence.

Gog became quite fond of the little mouse. He melted inside whenever their eyes locked, and he often wished that he could take his gnarled forefinger and gently pet Mr. Fellows' velvety coat. He was truly an endearing little rodent. But the gnome knew that the mouse was a wild creature from the woodlands and that he needed to respect his *wildness*. To try to make a pet of him would be a disservice, for eventually he would reunite with his own kind one day to resume his field-mouse life. And so, he resisted any attempt to get any closer to the little mouse. For now, Mr. Fellows was a very pleasant diversion for Gog, and the little mouse provided him with much happiness.

Whenever Gog either entered or departed from the lean-to, he was extremely careful in securing the door. He knew that his beloved companion Daniel could not be trusted around this new friend, and he certainly didn't want to inadvertently offer up Mr. Fellows as his cat's next meal. He decided it was best to treat the interior of the cottage and the little lean-to as two separate worlds, making sure that only he could bridge the gap between them.

Whenever Gog visited Mr. Fellows, he closely studied the little mouse's endearing features: his perky little ears, slick chestnut coat, and little curved tail. One day when the gnome walked in, he was delighted to see Mr. Fellows sitting within the light of a pale sunbeam that had come through a chink in the clapboard and on into the storeroom. The mouse was giving himself a tongue bath to freshen up his coat. He carefully combed his fur numerous times, and then he began to scrub his face with his front paws. As he scratched at a bothersome flea that he found near his left ear, a cold draft whistled through the lean-to—sending Gog's little friend quickly scurrying back to his warm nest in the jar.

One especially cold day, Gog went to retrieve the little saucer and found to his dismay that the delicacies that he had set out the previous night were totally untouched. This puzzled Gog, for this had never happened before.

"Perhaps I've been feeding Mr. Fellows so well that he has chosen to live for a day or two on what he has previously stored away. Perhaps he has caught a slight winter cold and is recuperating in his little glass-jar home. Maybe he has found the egress chink in the pantry wall that he first used for his entry, returning to his family in the forest. However, I don't think this is a real possibility because the woods are still covered in snow, and this last week has been unusually windy and bitter cold." A certain sadness assailed the old gnome, for he had come to view his guest as a friend, and now it appeared that he was gone.

"I just can't imagine where Mr. Fellows might be. I worry about him, and it's the not knowing that makes the dilemma far worse. I feel so helpless. If he has gotten into trouble, I might be able to help him. If he has chosen to be reunited with his family, I might feel some sense of relief. But wondering about my little friend's whereabouts leaves me anxious and confused."

Weeks later, as February was beginning to slowly soften into March, Gog went to the pantry in search of some seeds for early sowing. When he entered the still, cold room he noticed the faint, but terrible, odor of Death. He immediately began to search for its cause. After looking behind countless jars and upending many flower pots, he finally removed a wooden lid that half-covered a large, empty crock and peered down into its depths. His heart caught in his throat—for there, at the very bottom of the crock, lay the remains of poor Mr. Fellows. Evidently, he had scurried across the lid, been oblivious to the gaping crevasse beyond, and tumbled down into the abyss below. Not being able to scramble up the glazed sides of the crock had sealed his fate, and he had slowly died of starvation. He had met his doom alone. Gog shook his head sadly while tears rolled down his cheeks.

"I never heard his silent pleas for help, and now my friend is gone forever. His food remained in his saucer just inches from where he now lies; but it might as well have been miles away because he could not reach it. In the very midst of plenty, poor Mr. Fellows succumbed to want." Solving the mystery of Mr. Fellows' disappearance had answered his curiosity, but it had also added unwelcomed sadness to Gog's life.

Chapter 10
Thunder-Demon

Though gentle of nature most of the time, Gog was not immune to his very own demons. He too was occasionally tormented by the darkest misery known to man and the sometimes-biting anger that could accompany it. Injustice, cruelty, rejection, loneliness, and despair—real and imagined—were unwelcome visitors who sometimes lingered for days when they sought him out and heavily leaned upon his stooped shoulders, changing his world in one moment from brilliant color to a wash of monotone. The elderly gnome had battled these demons his entire life, and he could never fathom from whence they came.

"At these times, when Thunder-demon invades my space, he growls deep within me—pummeling my innards until I want to scream, gnash my teeth, or howl. Often Thunder-demon is unrelenting, and he will not take his ease until I beat my own head against a tree. Sometimes Thunder-demon only gently simmers within me, coiled like a sleeping, venomous snake that might choose to strike at any moment. I wait patiently for him to slither away when he finally decides to let go—returning me to my usually sunny self. I can never understand the purpose of his visits, and I'm never able to foretell when he might visit me again. Over the years, I have just learned to endure him the best I can upon his arrival and to quickly forget him once he has departed."

The demon could always be counted on to return, not often; but, as an unwanted guest occasionally turns up on one's doorstep— uninvited, unannounced, and unwilling to leave, this anger-personified visitor would remain with Gog until he was ready to go.

During these stressful times, Gog tried to remain cheerful, keep busy, and seek the Light. But sometimes this Darkness could not be avoided, and he found himself enduring much pain and emptiness until it eventually ceased without warning. It was so hard to determine a winning strategy for these demon-inspired visitations. Even lapsing into fervent prayer, thinking only good thoughts, and humming sweet melodies to himself while lying prostrate upon his bed failed to totally rout the unwanted visitor. He continually looked for new and creative ways to cure himself of these re-occurring confrontations—all in vain.

As a child, Gog's mother often helped him to combat these moods with her songs and her baking. Holding him on her lap, she would softly croon to him, mostly songs that spoke of love, ancient tales of folks who had once lived in a gentler world, or familiar nursery rhymes with which he was very familiar. The little gnome would sometimes sob with little restraint and shudder with the emotional pain that surrounded him and was caused by Thunder-demon.

Frequently, Selah left him lightly napping in his little bed, totally wrung out from his bout with his battle with his dark foe. She would bake him seeded honey cakes upon the hearth that would be served later with piping hot mint tea. When he had been comforted by the food and drink, she would enfold him in a mother's loving embrace and gently rock him with his head upon her breast. Her gentle presence always seemed to help erase the emotional scars left by the demon. Unfortunately, now that Selah was gone, it was up to Gog to do battle with the demon's Darkness on his own; and he always dreaded these confrontations.

As the years went by, Gog often wondered why he was being singled out for Thunder-demon's visitations. It just didn't make sense. One moment he would be going about his business in providing for himself by stocking his larder or gathering firewood; he might be meditating on the mysteries of the natural world as it whirled around him in all its fascinating shapes and colors; or he might be pondering his identity as a gnome, a lost soul, a seeker of knowledge and truth—when out of nowhere he would be struck by the menacing presence of this monster from the Darkness. And he always felt so unprepared.

"Part of me always seems to collapse from within upon the Thunder-demon's arrival. I am always so fear-struck at his approach because it scares me to death that this horror is happening to me all over again. I always hope and pray that it will stop immediately, and that I won't have to experience the hurt, the agony, and the despair that accompany each visit. But it never does. Oh, if I only possessed a magic sword with which I could slay my enemy, or a magic spell that could provoke him to disappear, or even a persuasive prayer that might be strong enough to prevent any future visitations from ever happening again. But I have never been so fortunate. Still, I endure; and I try to pretend that his most recent visit has finally been his last. And I go on living my life, trying not to let my dread of Thunder- demon's return spoil the many blessings that have been left upon my doorstep."

Gog could never understand the reason for the demon's visits. It seemed that there should be some rationale for why the good Lord forced him to endure this enemy's presence for as long as he could remember. Was he such a sinner that he deserved to be punished in such a way? Or was he so much of a believer and person of faith that his enemy wanted to continually test him with his insulting presence, forcing him to give in to the Darkness? He could only hope that his persecution was based on his faith!

Perhaps he was being punished for something he had done without his knowledge? An innocent mistake that was misunderstood and used forever against him? Gog wondered if he had been chosen at random, not necessarily by God but maybe by a cold and uncaring universe that doled out punishment and reward strictly based on chance. But this he dismissed out of hand because wasn't his Maker the creator of all that had been, was, and would ever be? Did a way exist in which he could battle Thunder-demon decisively so that he could avoid any more of these cruel confrontations in the future?

"Though I have thought about my circumstances my entire life, always seeking to avoid my confrontations with this dark one, I have yet to understand or find a solution to my dilemma. I have finally decided that the best I can do is promise myself that I will continue to endure these unwelcomed visits with love and grace, knowing that the Light is but moments away. A new dawn always seems to be waiting to be born shortly after Thunder-demon takes his leave, and my most current suffering soon becomes but a memory of yesterday."

Thankfully, Thunder-demon's visits appeared to be a bit less prevalent than in the past. Gog counted his blessings in this regard, for he no longer had the stamina he once had to withstand the punishment that came with these visits. Perhaps his advancing age had convinced Thunder-demon that the gnome was no longer a worthy opponent, and he no longer rated his time and presence as highly as he once had. Perhaps he had become bored with this gnome, who had been his plaything for so many years; and he had set out to find someone younger and more interesting to torment. There were no real answers—only questions about the where's and why's of an opponent who had made Gog's life miserable for decades.

However, whenever Thunder-demon did show up unannounced, his eventual departure would but heighten Gog's pleasure of the next day's brilliant sunrise as it tinted his home with its rosy glow. The pain caused seemed to be replaced almost immediately with a sense of euphoria, calm, and peace. A glow from the heavens seemed to bear witness to the end of torment and usher in the beginnings of unrestrained joy.

Gog pressed his nose to the window and felt his spirits lift as the evil presence began to disappear as quickly as it had come. He watched patiently for the first evening star and sighed with a sense of contentment.

"The world following a storm is newly-born. New beginnings are possible, and positive feelings stir the imagination. The metamorphosis from victim to victor gives many a butterfly fragile, but beautiful, wings with which to fly."

Upon Thunder-demon's most recent leave-taking, Gog was soon flipping pancakes on the griddle. Daniel rubbed up against him as he ladled a bit of honey with dried raspberries upon his early-morning breakfast. A sweet calm descended upon the cottage, and all was right with the world.

Chapter 11
Sentinel Of The Forest

As Gog sat upon the stone stoop in front of his cottage, he wove a reed mat for his doorway. He explored the intricate pattern of twists and turns in the mat that were created by his nimble fingers as they manipulated the flexible fibers. The intricate pattern seemed indicative of his life which had been designed by his Maker: complicated and rather difficult to maneuver, but carefully planned, sometimes short and sometimes long, smooth and rough, fragile yet durable. The doormat seemed almost capable of mapping out the twists and turns of his life. He sometimes wished that his life could be that predictable.

"I sometimes wonder about the why's, the what's, and the how's. I know that beings of thought spend much time pondering questions without answers, and I have always wondered why that was. Will there ever come a day when I might just wake up and live joyfully without being encumbered with worry and doubt about my life. Will there ever come a day when I might enjoy a glorious sunrise without acknowledging that a sunset must invariably follow? Will I ever be able to enjoy the present moment without encountering the shadows of the past and the mirages of the future?"

He set down the mat, and carefully examined it for sturdiness. The border had to be strong so that it would not fray. He wanted it to withstand the daily use of his comings and goings, sturdy enough to trap the mud and debris which he brought back with him from his tramps through the woods, but he also wished it to be a thing of beauty.

"Somehow," Gog continued to muse, "I have always felt that life is like swimming upstream in a vat of jelly: a journey in slow motion to an uncertain destiny. Perhaps that is why my mother was so intent upon living life in the present; it avoided so much pain and unnecessary questioning." Gog blinked in the harsh sunlight, donned his cap, and sought the shade of the nearby glen. His footsteps were rather slow and measured, for his mind was heavy with thought.

***

Occasionally there were days when Gog wished to leave his heavy burdens behind him. He hoped for nothing more than to have someone listen to the woes stored in his troubled mind and then to acknowledge them with a soothing and hopeful manner. For this Gog often sought counsel and reassurance from the sentinel of the forest, Quaking Aspen. Today was no different, and he went on his way deep into the woods to seek the best listener of all.

The shady path that Gog followed was strewn with leaves. He encountered an orange salamander, an orb spider, and a pure white toadstool as he walked steadily towards the center of the woods. As he approached his old friend Quaking Aspen, a venerable giant aspen beyond compare, the gentle rustlings from its leaves sifted through the glade, providing him with welcome.

Quaking Aspen towered above most of the other trees in the forest, his sturdy limbs and bountiful leaves completely shading the furthest bend of the path. His massive trunk was anchored by roots that spread deeply into the forest loam, and because of this Gog's friend had virtually no competition from neighboring trees or saplings who resided nearby. He had been able to flourish with all the nutrients, sunshine, and moisture that surrounded him, and his gigantic size was testament to that. This special tree had witnessed the many changes in the forest and the world around him for more than two hundred years, and he had growth rings to prove it. The aspen now looked down upon the gnome who stood below him, looking up to his friend with a bit of awe.

"Quaking Aspen, you've been here forever it seems. I never think about these woods without thinking about you. It's true that your height and width have naturally increased with age, and this has also increased the respect I pay you. Your presence is most definitely awe-inspiring."

Some of the tree's limbs had been lost or deformed by time and storm. The tree had begun to show the occasional fungus upon his trunk, his bark no longer had the healthy texture of a sapling, and more and more of his roots had come to the surface of the forest floor. Still, he remained a wise denizen of his forest domain, and its occupants continued to pay homage to him.

When the gnome visited his old friend, the tree whispered secrets to him in confidence through the crackling whisper of his leaves, and often he dipped his head to share further wisdom taken from the various other woodland sages that also lived there.

He stood tall, gray, and solemn. The flutter of his leaves was companionable, and they encouraged Gog to share some of the sorrows of his everyday life and seek a lightening of his soul. As Gog lay some of his burdens to rest at the doorstep of Quaking Aspen, he found that he was soon telling him about the many blessings and miracles that he had also experienced recently. As an inhabitant of the woodlands, his life was filled with goodness—as well as trials. Gog now realized that his burdens seldom outweighed his many blessings, and that the wise old tree seemed intent upon providing him with encouragement as he pointed out the balance, of both good and bad, that existed in his life.

This sentinel of the forest was a good friend to Gog, one who seemed always available when called upon for the telling of secrets and long, therapeutic sessions of conversation. Quaking Aspen gave long, drawn-out answers to Gog's many questions, though most were impossible to understand and interpret. The gnome, who quietly listened for hours, believed that he was receiving all the answers to the many questions of the universe if only he could be a better listener, enough so that he could but grasp the true meaning of the old tree's conversation. Gog desperately wanted to gather the wisdom that flitted to him with the flutter of leaves, but the tree's truths always seemed to escape him.

"I always gladly receive Quaking Aspen's sage advice, though my attempt to decipher his meaning seems to always fall short. Still— his wise counsel seems to comfort me, and he helps me to accept my many trials and tribulations. I believe that it is his very presence as a cherished friend that gives me confidence and helps me to carry on my own life, as imperfect as it is. I always leave him with the hope that perhaps on my next visit I will be more successful in translating his responses. I have never felt that my time with the aspen was ever wasted, for I have always left him feeling far more positive and inspired than before."

The tree's murmurings were often punctuated by birdsong, the clacking of branches, and the soughing of afternoon breezes. Gog would be lulled to sleep by the calming voices of Quaking Aspen and the other trees of the forest. His dreams that followed were always calm and soothing. He eventually awoke from his nap refreshed and relaxed—ready to make his trip back home to his cottage.

"My visits to my friend Quaking Aspen ease my troubled mind, not because my questions and concerns have necessarily been answered and my problems solved, but because my fears have been lightened. My friend has cared enough to listen and respond; and, though my friend is not a warm-blooded creature, still I am convinced that some sort of heart and soul are centered within him. I feel honored that he lives in woodland beyond my home."

Gog thought about how important it was for someone to have the patience to listen to him, to be heard without being judged. "I wonder if I am the very best listener that I can be. Listening is so important. Though I cannot understand Solomon's cheeps or Daniel's meows, it doesn't mean that I should not take the time to patiently listen to them. All creatures need to be given a voice, and their voices should be heard by one who genuinely cares about them."

***

Solomon, the little chickadee, was a compassionate listener, and he was greatly loved because of this. He had lived with Gog for many years, and the two had created a very close bond. The little bird often cocked his head and watched him with his sharp, black eyes whenever he approached. If the gnome fed him some tasty tidbits from the table, the chickadee always cheeped an appreciative thank-you.

"When I need someone to talk to, someone to alleviate my loneliness, or someone to relieve me of what is troubling me—I often turn to Solomon. I know that I can rely on him to listen to me, seriously acknowledge my presence, and provide me with support. The poor little bird lacks the ability to talk to me directly, yet I can feel his love and concern as clearly as the heat from the hearth's embers."

When called upon by Gog for his listening skills, Solomon cocked his perky head with the little black cap, directed his eyes to Gog's troubled brown eyes and wrinkled brow, and then perched as close to the side of his willow cage as possible. Not once during their session did the bird chirp or peck at his food. He always gave Gog his full attention because he could sense that a real need existed, and he and the gnome could not be the very best of friends if he did not step up his attempt to comfort his friend from time to time.

I know that I owe my life to Gog; but, of course, it is more than that. With only one wing, and the inability to care for myself, I want to be accepted as more than a liability—a crippled acquaintance. I really want to be recognized and needed for who I am as a friend. It's important for me to contribute to the well-being of those within the walls of this little cottage in the woods. Being a supportive friend is a small price to pay for feeling that my life has some importance.

It seemed that it all came down to that—compassionate listening. When love and support were freely given, life seemed far less cold and harsh. When friends cared enough to give of themselves and their time, they provided a soft cushion for the daily hurts sometimes found in life.

Gog wished Solomon a pleasant *good night*, and then he stirred the embers on the hearth, added three chunks of wood, and put the kettle on for a cup of hot tea. Soon the little cottage was warm and cozy as the heat from the fireplace radiated throughout. He picked up **The Good Book** and began to read—continuing to search for answers.

Chapter 12
Metamorphosis

Gog had always been fascinated with the ability of things to change, whether it was the weather, seasons, the growth of offspring, colors of the trees, or the appearance of some things—like rain turning to snow. Changes in personality, temperament, and outlook were also fascinating changes to recognize in a creature's character. You could experience a change of fortune. You might realize you had changed your direction in life. Or you could decide to change your life's goals. But when change became so complete, awe-inspiring, and beautiful that a creature's very outward appearance along with its very presence, motor skills, and inner workings were changed; Gog couldn't help but be overcome by total wonderment. This kind of change the gnome knew as metamorphosis because it was complete and so very, very special.

Metamorphosis involved the total rebirth of a rather simple creature into something that seemed far more breathtaking and complex. The new, totally improved, creature seemed to be an accomplishment of Heaven, for it seemed far more beautiful and accomplished than the old creature. It had become an exquisite, new creation. Gog had witnessed firsthand how pollywogs became frogs, grubs became cicadas, eggs became ducklings, and caterpillars became moths and butterflies. He had often experienced these changes himself in his own woodland habitat, and he recognized them as miracles of metamorphosis.

Gog had learned much about metamorphosis from the many Monarch butterflies that flitted through the sunlit glen that skirted his woods. These colorful *fairies* drifted through the patches of sunlight in the meadows surrounding his woodland. They sought sweet flower nectar and pollen to sustain their energy for their extravagant flights, and they had held him spellbound since his days as a child. When the butterflies first arrived in the summer months, the gnome celebrated their return with a wide smile. They seemed like such peaceful, carefree souls whose lives consisted of gently winging their way through the woodland, randomly flitting from flower to flower.

Gog's brow furrowed, and he seemed to contemplate something both mysterious and serious. "I know there is far more to Monarch butterflies than meets the eye. I have studied them as a friend and scholar my entire life. I have learned so much about their life cycles by being both aware and curious. The butterflies continue to teach me about how important it is to prepare for any change. I know that they are meant as a life lesson; but I have failed to totally grasp what lesson it is that I should grasp."

"In early autumn, many Monarchs flit through my glen on their way to some unknown destination. They seek the patches of milkweed that grow there. Their meetings with these plants take place during the transitional period when the summer season bridges fall. Though the butterflies hover above the glen for only a matter of days, it is never long before delicate crescents appear upon many milkweed leaves. These crescents are carved by the visitors' larval offspring, voracious black and green striped caterpillars that hatch from eggs that had been laid on the milkweed leaves. The caterpillars assuage their rampant hunger with the abundance of the milkweed leaves. The next generation of Monarch butterflies is already intent on change."

"The main purpose of the Monarch larvae is extremely simple: they are meant to gorge themselves on tender milkweed leaves from morning until night. It is a feast that must continue, uninterrupted, for days. The caterpillars always grow so quickly that I can almost see them grow with my very own eyes. One day they are no bigger than the moon on my thumbnail, but within days they measure the entire length of my thumb itself. Soon these worms become rather round, and their bodies stretch to almost an inch and a half in length. And still they munch, and munch, and munch!"

"Their munching continues until, at last, they tire of this endless gorging; and not able to find a comfortable couch upon which they can rest their over-stuffed bodies, they attach themselves with a tiny silken thread to the underside of a milkweed stalk or nearby vegetation that might provide them with even better camouflage. There they hang—suspended over the abyss of life, waiting."

"Almost immediately, it seems, the ugly worm becomes totally transformed. In its place, a brilliant emerald-green jewel etched with magnificent gold tracings is to be found, hanging suspended in midair as if a magician has pulled off a miraculous slight-of-hand—from larva to a chrysalis in an overnight fete of magic. What now appears looks a bit like an exaggerated version of an acorn—an acorn that aspires to become a precious jewel one day. However, the chrysalis's most miraculous change will be far more stunning than even that."

Gog scoured the milkweed, looking for a sign of the coming "grand change." He hoped to be able to view the pending metamorphosis when a butterfly would finally emerge from its chrysalis at the appropriate time, but he was always too late to bear witness to this miracle. Brilliant Monarch butterflies magically appeared where jeweled chrysalises had once been just the day before, and the newly-hatched butterflies could be seen gracefully drying their wings in preparation for their first flights. Their opaque, bright-orange wings seemed to catch fire in the dayglow; and they flaunted their new selves in the day glow—like Icarus, preparing for flight towards the sun, but having wisely chosen gossamer wings instead of wax.

Gog could not ignore his disappointment in missing the spectacular metamorphosis in person. Time and time again he arrived too late. Finally, he began to place a caterpillar in a glass canning jar with a ventilated lid. He filled the jar with milkweed stalks that supported the choicest leaves, tender and moist. Then he watched spellbound for the next few days as the worm binged on the tender leaves, continuously eating as his body grew and grew and grew.

"I watch with interest and amazement, taking note of the many miraculous changes that are taking place within my homemade terrarium. My quick-change artist is a famished caterpillar one day, striped black and green; and the next day he is gone—replaced by an elegant spring-green chrysalis etched in gold."

"When I finally glimpse this jewel of a chrysalis hanging suspended on its silken thread, I know that it will not be long before I will see the miracle of metamorphosis before my very own eyes." Gog smiled softly as he reminisced about the birthing process of the Monarch butterfly.

"As the day for the miracle approaches, I keep a close watch. The chrysalis itself darkens, and the once-brilliant green gem becomes an almost insignificant coal-black husk. I know that the 'birthing' is about to take place. Finally, a new creature breaks free from its confinement, and emerges to its new life. A scrunched-up butterfly, crinkled and damp, has taken the place of the caterpillar that once lived within. It seems to be so much larger than the husk from which it has just recently broken free. It hangs with but an imperceptible flutter as it waits for its wings to dry—gradually becoming accustomed to the freedom of space."

"The new butterfly, with slight movement and gentle tremors, gradually flexes it wings to test the world around it. When it finally opens its wings to their fullest and begins to flutter in earnest—seeking the freedom of blue sky, I know that I must quickly release it so that it can become part of the great world beyond. Sometimes it will cling precariously to one of my gnarled fingers for initial support, until is prepared to make its first foray. I watch the Monarch as it slowly flutters away, gradually gaining altitude. Its orange and black stained-glass wings seem to be accented by the azure backdrop of an autumn sky. I have most certainly witnessed a miracle!" Gog sighed, and his heart seemed full to breaking.

"I always hold my breath when I accompany each newborn *fairy* to my doorway, its slender legs perched precariously on my gnarled finger. The grandeur and beauty of this new creature never fails but to hold me spellbound. I watch in delight as its fragile wings grant it flight, and it flutters aloft to join its own kind airborne or sets off to locate a bloom for its first sip of nectar."

"Metamorphosis. It is truly a miraculous concept! Even when studying this fascinating event as a scholar might, I cannot help but wonder at this miraculous change in a creature's existence that takes place in such a short period of time. I cannot begin to imagine what each of these insects feels as it changes from a voracious caterpillar gorging on milkweed one day, then to a worm encased in a precious jewel, and finally transforming into a most magnificent butterfly ready for its first grand flight."

Gog most certainly felt a kinship with the hungry green caterpillar that spent its days munching milkweed, mindlessly filling its belly with cellulose, not fully realizing the importance of its diet and what was to come.

"If a caterpillar transforms itself in a matter of days to something as wondrous as a colorful butterfly, is it not possible for a similarly extravagant change to occur for someone like me as well? I often feel that my earthly body might very well be just a shell that encases something special growing within me, something miraculous that is just biding its time. Perhaps it is a spiritual me that also wishes to soar to Heaven above. Truly, metamorphosis might be possible for even a simple creature such as myself, a simple woodland gnome." Gog certainly prayed that it was so.

"To have the ability to make such a transition is something that I can only dream about, for I realize that it would take much heavenly intervention. The Monarch butterfly, a creation of the Maker, finds itself able to go from the very ordinary to the very extraordinary in just a matter of days—in a most wondrous way. It seems to claim metamorphosis as a natural right, whereas my heavenly petition might be merely just a wish at this point."

"It seems to me that in one breathless moment the butterfly severs its earthly ties when it flexes its wings in preparation for its very first flight, so that it can soar as a *fairy* to the very heights of treetops where it may mingle with sunbeams and glide upon heavenly breezes. It goes almost immediately from munching milkweed leaves to sipping nectar from flowers. How miraculous is that? It has truly experienced a divine change that makes me sigh with a bit of envy and much longing."

There was something that remained deep inside the gnome that dared him to believe that his hope of a grand metamorphosis could exist for even him—an earthbound, rather ugly bit of primitive mankind. Over the years as he released butterfly after butterfly into the world beyond, Gog often imagined himself a passenger on those many wings; and for the briefest of moments he too felt that he could fly to the heavens beyond on the backs of these celestial beings.

Chapter 13
Pilgrimage To The Sea

One day, just before dawn, Gog sat upon his stoop with Daniel by his side. He had risen early just to see the sunrise. "First comes the presence of day, the world's inhalation—followed by the presence of night, the world's exhalation. To me, the world's opposites are symbolized by day and night, a balance of cosmic proportions."

The very heartbeat of life was powerful, and Gog often listened to its sounds: splendid outpourings of croaks, mutterings, muted cries—chirpings, stirrings, and uttered sighs. He dreamt of the music of a song sparrow floating through ferny forests that blossomed with mushrooms and woodbine. As he waited for the first rosy rays of the new dawn, he took a deep breath and centered his thoughts on the world around him.

"The leaf mold that speaks of Death is silent, but it frequently gives voice to exotic woodland perfumes that blend with the fragrances of pine, mint, and wild roses. A gentle lull of blessed peace laps at my soul, acting like a balm; and I think of Selah, my mother, as she is with me—in my mind and in my heart. I feel her arms around me, and I am her child once again: inhaling the fragrance of honeysuckle from her apron and feeling her breath as she kisses the top of my head. I remember her as a young woman bending over to pick a bouquet of buttercups, yarrow, and ferns. I can hear her voice, sometimes little more than a lilting whisper, as it comforts me or sings a lullaby. Now her soul's green light flickers in the bottle on my table. It is her very essence that glows within. She is still alive—and present—in my life. Yet, she is not."

A clap of thunder dispelled the dream just as cymbals disrupt a stirring overture. Gog was alone, and he felt the chill of the coming storm sink deep into his bones. He pulled his hat down tighter around his head and buttoned his coat, hoping to reach his cottage before he was overtaken by the storm. As he approached his home, Daniel the bobcat scurried through the cottage door and leapt up upon the bed.

The pitter patter of raindrops on the predawn forest floor was hypnotic, soothing, and gentle. The rain awakened peace and hope within the gnome while washing away his grief and sadness. However, the early sunrise which he had anticipated had been destroyed by the rainy weather. His spirits plummeted a bit, and he was disappointed when the sun's rosy beams disappeared and the silver, encroaching fog set about to running its fingers through the boughs of the trees and shrubbery now drenched with rain.

***

Occasionally seeking adventure, answers, and company in solitude—Gog tramped through the woods, hoping to calm his troubled mind with the comfort he might find there. "It is very difficult, this living my life alone without the loving connection I had come to cherish. Most never realize how important companionship and conversation truly are. Being able to communicate with another as to what passes through the mind in the hopes of finding common ground, problems often find solutions, and a sharing of memories strengthens a relationship. Everything I do now, I do alone—except for events in my daily life which I may sometimes share with my woodland friends."

"It is true that my Solomon and Daniel provide me with some solace from loneliness, but it is never enough. We may share food at mealtimes and the comforting knowledge that we are not alone when we fall asleep. We provide each other with a bit of company and the sounds that arise as we go about living our communal lives. Our languages are so dissimilar that our communication is minimal, and we cannot ever arrive at the closeness found between family members and friends of a similar nature. Perhaps it is time for me to travel away from my home to shake these doldrums and gain a new perspective."

Gog was constantly seeking to learn, understand, and appreciate himself, the natural world around him, and the creatures that inhabited it. He finally decided that a pilgrimage to the sea would give him the opportunity to expand his level of understanding—finding and exploring a world far different from the woodland environment where he lived. His loneliness was beginning to eat him alive, for his cottage lacked the true companionship that he craved. He was still spry enough and retained the endurance required for a rather long, strenuous walking tour; and he decided that he most definitely needed a change of pace. For years he had read about the sea, thought about the sea, and dreamed about the sea. He finally decided that it was time to take it upon himself to make a pilgrimage to the sea in person, no matter how long and difficult the journey.

Gog went about preparing the cottage so that Solomon and Daniel would have access to plenty of food and water while he was gone. They would have each other for company, the door to the summer kitchen now stood open and a cat box had been installed for Daniel, and the little cottage would provide all the comfort and security that they needed while Gog was away. He knew that they would miss him, just as he would miss them. But after preparing his home to meet their basic needs without him for a few weeks of survival on their own, he bid them good-bye and hoisted his haversack upon his back. He was traveling light, for he was used to getting along on very little; and he certainly didn't need excess weight to carry on his journey. He would rely on his Maker's care and mercy while on his journey, for he had decided that his self-sufficiency while away was an important part of his pilgrimage. He was determined to learn more about this world in which he lived, and he would do it on his own terms.

For days Gog travelled towards the east in the direction of the sea, so that he could finally experience in life what he had imagined in dreams for so long. The journey was arduous. Gog relied on mushrooms, berries, and creek salads for his sustenance. He drank deeply of the cold spring water that he found spurting out of rocky fissures. During the day he walked for miles, though his pace was rather slow but determined. And in the evening, he covered himself with tree boughs and slept under the stars. Not once did he ever consider that perhaps this venture might be ill-advised or impossible.

The days stretched into weeks. Solomon and Daniel having been left secure in the cottage, still invaded Gog's mind from time to time. Though they had plenty to eat and drink, still—they would miss him and happily reunite with him upon his return. Gog did not plan to spend much time at the seaside once he arrived, for just reaching it and experiencing it were key factors in the purpose of his journey. He knew that his return trip would take far less time and be far more direct. Now, however, he was savoring the pilgrimage.

As Gog came closer to his destination, the first thing that he saw was a row of rather ominous-looking storm clouds. They had soaked up much moisture from the sea and accumulated electricity from the rocky shoreline. The storm clouds dueled for a brief time with flashes of lightning and rumbles of thunder, but their battle was short-lived for the air was still relatively cool and quickly diminished their strength.

The clouds soon began to shift and disappear; and a brilliant sunrise arose, immersing the horizon in brilliant color. With the visibility much improved, Gog finally saw the sea in all its glory.

"The sea is positively massive! Why, it stretches for as far as my eyes can see! It looks like a shiny turquoise blanket that reflects each ray of sunlight, dazzling my eyes with color and light. It shimmers and twinkles as the sun's rays dance upon its surface as if it hides the light of Glory within its very depths. I cannot believe that I am really standing here, looking down upon it. This feels far too much like a dream, yet my senses are alive with the sight of it, the sound of it, the smell of it."

Gog took a deep breath of the foreign-smelling air and then quickly exhaled. He looked puzzled as he thought about this new experience. "The air reminds me of fish, swamp mud, and clean clothes from the stream—all at once! The smell is very, very different; but strangely, it is not unpleasant. In fact, it is a bit heady, exhilarating, and quite pleasing. It makes me feel so happy to be alive!"

Gog's attention was soon drawn to the booming sounds of the large waves that rolled and crashed against the cavernous shore, gently scrubbing it with foam and bubbles. "The waves along the shore seem positively alive! They rollick like very loud, exuberant creatures who wish to play as their momentum is constantly repeated along the shore. I feel the sea's heart pulse in rhythm with the loud crashes of its waves that boom and echo. The presence of the rows upon rows of waves is overwhelming! They swamp the shore time and time again with flood water that swiftly retreats in gentle ripples. I have never seen anything quite like it! There is a real part of me that feels as if I must have once been some part of this gigantic body of water, for it seems to call to me as no other wonder in this world ever has."

When Gog reached the sea's edge, he quickly took off his shoes and rolled up his pants. He was anxious to feel the temperature and energy of this gigantic body of water that mesmerized him with its all-encompassing presence.

"When I strode into the waves, I was delighted by the sharp cold that instantly met me at its shore. The waves lapped at my feet, and I shivered at the icy cold that could stop a man's heart. I had tasted its salty nature, now I felt its stickiness that was immersed in each wave; and I smelled the pungent spray that pervaded the entire coast with the fragrance of fish, seaweed, and roiling water. It was so invigorating!"

"The seductive pull of the waves, as they headed back to sea—having just recently crashed upon the shore, was both exciting and intimidating. This unchained power of this, God's mighty creation, seemed to warn me that I could soon be vanquished by it if I chose to swim too far from its shore."

Gog quickly hurried down to the beach, eager to explore these new surroundings. He was astounded at the co-mingling of soft sand and seawater, ankle-deep and alive with surge; rocks of all shapes and sizes, knife-sharp and softly rounded smooth; the fascinating driftwood sculptures abandoned on the shoreline, polished silver by the undulating wind and waves; and the beautiful, artistically decorated seashells, delicately scalloped or pristine white with little if any decoration.

The gnome plodded through the sand, navigating around the many rocks and pools of water, eager to explore the seashore for the very first time. He was impatient to discover for himself some of the treasures that he had been told lay beneath the sea's salty billows as well as upon the shore. As he walked along the water's edge, studying the magnificence of the rolling waves before him, his attention was diverted by the seaweed, sea creatures, and seabirds, both dead and alive, that could be found along the strand, in the air, or in the shallow waves. In the tidal pools he soon discovered treasures that completely took his breath away.

"I find jellies and streamers and saucers of many textures and colors. I am overwhelmed by the diversity of the many sea creatures. I had assumed that there would be an assortment of fish, but I had not dreamed of such a variety of seaweeds, diverse creatures that both crawl and swim, and the random display of beautiful shells that are scattered all about. And I continue to be astounded by the movement, power, and music of the sea."

Gog began to synthesize the many thoughts and emotions about his perceptions of the sea through poetry:

Turquoise essences drift in waves of motion—
emitting little sound, much surge, and no trace.
Dollops of light flash in cataclysmic resonance,
mirroring rainbows that converge, swell, and then fade.
The dazzle never leaves the eye,
and the mystification of it all is indelible.
Surrealism becomes more real than a pulse.

Gog was entranced by all that he saw, and he sat upon the shore with his bare toes curled into the cool, wet sand for hours. He was mesmerized by the crash of the waves and the gentler melody of the ebb and flow of the receding waters. He licked at the salt upon his lips, closing his eyes as he savored it. He had lived his entire life away from the sea, and only now could he begin to understand the magnitude of what he had missed during all those years.

"I never realized that my odyssey to see and experience the sea would eventually lead me to so many other-worldly delights. These delights are totally beyond comparison to anything else that I have ever known in my own world. Though I have not had one sip of my dandelion wine, sitting by this massive, living ocean— I feel that I have drunk near half a bottle. I feel overcome by all the wonder of this unbelievably mystical world. It beckons me to stay and become part of it, but I know that the temptation is not real— and definitely not fitting for the life of a woodland gnome."

"The powerful existence of the waves cannot be denied and, in their salt-water swells I find constant motion, make many discoveries, and learn important lessons. Here at the sea, I am reminded of the miracle of creation, and I think of my Maker who is responsible for it all. I realize that the waves share a common thread with God, for their ominous power is constant, unpredictable, and far beyond man's control as are His. I value how the sea has made me recognize my insignificance and vulnerability as a mere mortal, a speck of sand amidst God's creations. And as daunting as that may seem, I may still count upon his very personal love and direction for me."

"How I will cherish this pilgrimage to the sea! Though solving mysteries may seem to belong to the everyday world, it does not have to necessarily be that way. Our lives may be relegated to the earthbound, and it may sometimes feel that our wings have been clipped and our ankles shackled. However, that may not be necessarily true for all. For those who choose to courageously ride the wind currents of life like the seagulls, there may be creativity, imagination, and even eternity . . ."

Gog sat down upon a sand dune. His thoughts drifted to his new experiences at the sea, and he felt inspired to give voice to them:

Time is fluid like the sea.
It surges and waits for no bark,
No pilot.
Love is effervescent,
Its bubbles—heartbreakingly precious.
It too rides the tide . . .
And often never returns.
Always waiting for the big wave,
The wave that will return it to shore
With incredible beauty and delight.

Gog's pilgrimage to the sea had truly been eye-opening. The world beyond his rather limited glen had expanded his mind far beyond anything he could have ever imagined. He had beheld the remarkable sea—a living, breathing thing. He had seen its creatures, smelled its fragrance, tasted its salt, touched its volatility, and heard its rhythm and pulse. What had started as a quest to feed the hunger of a lifelong curiosity had ended in a deeper appreciation and understanding of another world, and in turn—his own world. And it had also led him back to his Maker once again.

"I amassed so many delightful memories of watching the gulls dip and dive for their dinner on shore and in the waves. I'll always remember deeply inhaling the heady concoction of salt spray, fish, and bayberry. I'll never forget my many visits to the tidal pools, which were filled with stranded sea creatures and seaweed that had been left behind by thoughtless waves. I can remember frantically flinging many of them back into the churning waves, my desperate attempt to rescue these helpless, dying creatures—returning them back to the sea in the hope that they might survive for another day. One day I pocketed a perfect purple shell as a remembrance of my visit, and I even chewed a slimy piece of seaweed just to experience its taste."

"Though my adventure will stay with me for a lifetime, it also proved to me that the woodland is truly my home. It's where I belong. While away from it, I grieved a bit over my separation from my daily life. Living my life, recalling my many memories, and imagining all my hopes and dreams—all take place there. At the side of the sea, I truly felt very small and insignificant—even more alone. The comfort I had come to expect in my cottage, and in the woods, meadows, and swampy land that surround it, was not to be found near the impersonal echo of the crashing waves."

Traveling to the sea had provided Gog with true spiritual and philosophical inspiration, urging him to explore his own existence further, but it had also heightened the pleasure he experienced upon his own homecoming. After a quick though arduous journey home, he finally stepped into the clearing surrounding his cottage. He was overcome by emotion.

"I am home. It is here that I truly feel a bond to God and His Son. I am not distracted by the new, the foreign, or the different. I have a glorious sense of myself as a believer of the eternity I one day hope to inherit. I draw inspiration from the very trees, shrubs, and plants that surround my cottage for my life's work. Walking through the door of my cottage, I inhale the fragrance of *home*, and I feel a true sense of belonging. My home is more than a scant few acres of habitat and a shelter; it is a cosmic point in time and place that helps to identify who I am. I am Gog, the last gnome of these woodlands."

Upon his return, tears welled up in the gnome's eyes. The vine-covered cottage had never looked dearer to him. Being reunited with Solomon and Daniel proved to him that, though his friends were lacking in gnome-like qualities, they were able to show excitement and love upon his return. Their endearing *cheeps* and *purrs* were welcoming and touched his heart. Later, when Gog sat at the table—his home illuminated by a crackling fire and a newly-lit candle, his heart leapt with joy and thanksgiving; for once again he had recaptured a sense of belonging and a bit of calm amongst the storm of life.

The homecoming supper that evening celebrated the joyful reunion of a gnome and his two beloved cottage friends.

And, most importantly, the bottle that sat upon his table where he had left it when he had undertaken his journey to the sea—was still there in all its glory. The green glimmer cast by Selah's soul within the bottle remained steady and constant. Though its presence was a reminder to Gog of his deepest sins, it also comforted him and shed Light upon him.

***

When Gog occasionally visited his long-ago childhood life from time to time in dreams, he often consulted his memories from his once-in-a-lifetime excursion to the sea as well. The sights and sounds had brought about an epiphany of sorts, providing his soul with much growth and food for thought for the many days to come.

Memories were becoming increasingly more important to the gnome as his life settled back into the habit of merging with the seasons. He now took the time to explore both the every-day and the ordinary, along with the expected. He worked longer hours to sustain both body and soul in his own life's struggle, and to prepare himself for the unexpected.

When Selah had lived by his side, Gog's existence had been rather comfortable. Loneliness never seemed to be an issue. The aromas of simmering stews and baking breads permeated the cottage. Cobwebs and dust bunnies were briskly swept away. And the fire on the hearth, more-often-than-not, merrily snapped and crackled as it licked the logs with flame. He had been surrounded by a sense of *home*; and he had wallowed in what it was to be loved, pampered, and protected.

Deep down inside, Gog had always known that this fairy tale existence could not last forever. However, he had also known that it would be unwise to ruin the preciousness of it by giving in to excessive, constant worry. He had enjoyed his life then, and he would continue to do so now.

"I know that just as the morning sky greets the new day with color and light, I can always predict that at the end of the day the twilight may usually settle with a brooding darkness that not even twinkling stars can dissipate. But I have learned to enjoy my blessings as I receive them. I choose not to relish them to the exclusion of the world's sorrows, but I refuse to let these sorrows rule my every waking moment. Life is too short. And even the twilight can sometimes offer beauty and serenity. I must remind myself to always look for the good in life."

Chapter 14
The Neighborhood Meeting Place

At the back of the clearing in which the cottage was located, Gog had established a very informal compost pile. All the food scraps from his daily life found their way there. Everything from moldy biscuits to potato peelings and rotten tomatoes were thrown on this pungent heap. He also scattered animal bones, entrails, and hide in this rather unsightly mess. He occasionally turned over this heap with his fork while the creatures of the forest and the mealy worms continued to dine on these tasty leftovers.

The rich soil that would eventually be produced here and then used for his garden in the spring was beneficial, but the compost pile itself had become far more than that. It had become the neighborhood meeting place for many of the woodland creatures as well. Times were often lean in the forest, especially over the long winter months. Many animals had to search the countryside far and wide to find something to fill their bellies to keep hunger at bay. By the time the icy winds approached, the fruits and berries had all disappeared, worms and insects were all but non-existent, and snow with patches of ice covered the ground. Times of scarcity were now a reality. The compost pile drew many creatures to it like a magnet, for it offered sustenance in a time of need.

Gog enjoyed sharing the leftovers with his many neighbors. This array of scraps seemed to be a veritable feast for many who had come very close to starvation. The leftovers from Gog's table were more than welcomed in a landscape where frigid temperatures now dipped low enough to freeze tree limbs and running water, where the sun valiantly continued to distribute light that was reflected by the mounds of snow and ice but was no longer capable of generating heat.

Blue jays, a few nuthatches, and the ever-present chickadees were a few of the familiar birds that chose to visit the compost pile over the course of each day. They assembled to industriously pick at the fat and meat-encrusted bones that may have been exposed by hungry raccoons and skunks that visited the night before. Though the gathering could sometimes seem a bit competitive at times, in the end it always seemed a rather merry assembly that gathered to search for an easy meal during this time of hardship—a social event of long standing where sustenance could be frequently found.

A pair of midnight-black ravens always visited the compost pile at the crack of dawn. They were probably two of Gog's favorite visitors. They would boldly swoop in together, survey the food selection in the compost bin in from of them, and then position themselves next to some of the choicest leavings. Because they visited at dawn, their meals would often be frozen solid. They would have to attack their frozen breakfasts with their sharp beaks in order to eat it or transport it in manageable pieces, but they were always up for the challenge. Gog was fascinated by their antics and boisterous, deep-throated conversations.

"Aris and Avis, my resident ravens, are constantly on hand to pick away at the most tantalizing of my leavings, especially in the dead of winter. They are early risers, and I often wake up to their raucous cries when the ghostly fingers of dawn have just begun to filter through the wintry glen. They are hardy souls; and they are very often the first ones there to enjoy the feast and supervise those waiting to join them."

Gog often watched and commented on the antics of the crowd at the compost pile from the comfort of his home as he peered through a frost-rimed window, "The ravens are long-time scavengers; and they have overseen the compost pile for many, many years—feasting themselves or picking through it for transport. They will sometimes gorge themselves on leftovers right on the spot, or they will select a bone, especially one thick with skin and meat, and then fly away with it to store it up high in the crotch of a nearby tree where they can leisurely pick away at it later in the day."

However, the birds, and an occasional skunk or raccoon, were not the only woodland creatures to take note of the bounty of the compost pile. One day, at the very beginning of February, a striking red fox appeared in Gog's backyard. He casually trotted over to the pile, selected a choice partridge leg bone, and then wandered away. He was a young male, resplendent in his bright red fur coat—possessing all the grace, beauty, and vitality of a prime specimen of his species. Gog was immediately mesmerized.

"Against the backdrop of the fresh, white snow he positively glows—a splash of bright copper red on the sparkling white landscape. The fox shows absolutely no fear, and little hesitation. I am completely fascinated by his visit." Gog continued to survey the compost pile even more closely the next few days because he didn't want to miss another possible visit by the fox.

Weeks passed, winter finally begrudgingly melted into spring, and the fox remained in the area surrounding Gog's cottage where he had become a constant shadow. His visits to the compost pile became part of his daily routine. One day, as spring burst forth with birdsong and blossoms, Gog watched the young fox as he dug a hole at the perimeter of the compost pile.

"While digging his hole, the fox cocks his head—listening intently. He hears something and then quickly roots it out and grasps it with his teeth. He holds a mole within his jaws; and then he casually tosses it into the air, snaps its neck, and then proceeds to bury it back in the pile. He then goes back to digging again. He digs another hole, finds another mole, but proceeds to quickly eat this one—seeming to swallow it whole with little if any chewing. He sits down, stretches, scratches for fleas, and in general makes himself right at home. Eventually he wanders off. I suppose everything he does is just routine for his species, but I can't help but be fascinated by his antics, as blood-thirsty as they may appear."

Later in the season when Gog decided to explore the woods for dandelion and cowslip greens, he saw a splotch of color beneath a towering white pine. Dappled by the faint spring sun, the red fox calmly lay abed. It certainly seemed that he had chosen Gog's backyard for his own, staking claim to the hollows and hummocks where he could escape rain, bed down in comfort for the night, and survey the surrounding area in watchfulness.

Gog was amazed that the fox had chosen his neighborhood for his home territory. Evidently, he was not so reclusive that he would not choose to live close to others, nor was he so shy that he did not allow for some visual contact—though it was often limited and brief. The gnome sensed that he had been greatly honored by the fox for choosing to live his life so close to his. Rogue, as Gog later began to call him, became a constant presence in the dell.

He was indeed a wild creature that maintained his distance, but his life soon easily meshed with Gog's. When Gog made his trips into the woods, the fox often followed discreetly at a distance behind him. Wary, but thirsty for companionship, the fox would frequently slink through the trees and brush, always keeping Gog in sight. Another loner, this young male fox was most likely no longer welcomed by a mother who had evidently moved on to concerns for her younger kits. Now perceived as a young adult, Rogue had most probably been forced to move out to make room for his younger siblings; and from now on he would have to provide for himself. He had chosen to adapt to independence gradually by taking advantage of the site of Gog's cottage, which provided him with some easy meals as well as shelter.

Too young to establish his own fox family, too old for being adopted into another den, and too wild to be fully dependent on man—he was now struggling for a foothold in the world and for a sense of belonging, not knowing what that really meant or where it might lead him. On his own, he had chosen Gog and his world for that sense of place.

"I am absolutely delighted to welcome Rogue as one of my own, though I often warn Daniel to keep his distance as *cat*, even bobcat, occasionally appeals to the appetite of a very hungry fox—even one who appears so well-behaved. He is a handsome fellow, and a smart one too, and I must say that I enjoy his companionship on our tramps."

A strange, new friendship had been kindled, and it often filled Gog with awe. This connection that had been forged between a wild woodland creature and his chosen woodland gnome seemed almost magical. Though both shared the bond of existence within the same space, their differences were far more numerous than their similarities. Yet, they were frequently in tune to one another in many other ways. This constantly amazed Gog.

"We both take pleasure in sauntering down the paths of the forest at dawn as the birds are just beginning their morning songs.

We are both constantly on the alert for any and all opportunities regarding finding our own food for the day. We use our own techniques when we hunt but remain determined to locate our own meals on our walk. We quench our thirsts in the cool, dark pool by Quaking Aspen, taking our time to examine our own mirror image in it. And we both take naps during the heat of the day in the dense shade of the sugar maple by the brook."

These new friends seemed comforted by the companionship that they provided to one another. They also appeared entertained and thoroughly amused by some of the actions or mannerisms each exhibited. Their very differences fascinated them.

Gog sat down upon his backyard stoop this day to immerse himself in the mood of the meadow and forest. He looked around and thought about many of the observations that he had made throughout the years pertaining to the passage of the seasons and the interplay of the many creatures as they adapted to this constant change. He had been an avid student and had learned so much about nature by paying strict attention to its constant whims and temperaments.

"The animals of the woodland may seem far less burdened by a thinking mind than I am, and their ties to the many lives that go on around them may seem to have fewer intellectual and emotional ties to them. However, I am never really sure whether these distinctions might just be totally underestimated."

Gog scratched his head and then replaced his cap. He bent down and picked up his basket of vegetables, freshly gathered from the garden, and his cauldron. Soon he was diligently shelling peas, one of the first crops to be harvested for his dinner table. A rhythmic *plink, plink, plink* could be heard as the peas hit the sides of the cast iron pan. This day his basket also contained spring onions and spinach, and he would soon prepare these for his dinner as well.

"I've often witnessed animals, especially Rogue, my beloved fox, in what seems to be very thoughtful moods. I've often wondered if his life is quite as simple and guileless as I'm led to believe. Sometimes when I look deeply into Rogue's eyes, or into Daniel's or Solomon's, I have been startled by what I consider to be a sense of true understanding, and perhaps even a keen intelligence. Maybe I have simply under-estimated their intellectual powers. In fact, at times I'm sure of it."

Gog looked over at the young fox, and he thought about all he had learned of his new friend. They had spent much time in one another's company. Their silences had often been companionable and filled with a sense of appreciation for the time they shared together. Their lives seemed to mesh in such a way that their friendship did not conflict with their independence. Yet their ability to communicate, without a common language, was always implied rather than understood.

The gnome shook his head in disappointment. "Unfortunately, I am forced to admit that language, especially when it is not commonly shared by those who are unable to speak, provides a barrier which is almost impossible to break through. It has always kept our two worlds apart; and it will most likely continue to do so. I am convinced that very often birds and animals may understand what we say, especially if we keep it short and simple. But as for their ability to respond back to us—it just does not exist, except perhaps in the most discreet of facial gestures and primitive vocal noise."

Gog frowned as he thought about this barrier that separated him from his friends. He knew that so much of his loneliness might easily be erased in his day-to-day life if only he had the ability to converse with those closest to him. Unfortunately, the world he lived in did not allow him to draw closer to any of these friends because of this language barrier between them that was totally impenetrable. And because he was now one of a kind, this fact truly caused him a great deal of grief and loneliness.

"Unless I can miraculously learn to decipher the twitters, yowls, and barks of some of the birds and animals; or can translate the subtle body language that accompanies their every movement, and they in turn can learn to interpret what my speech may imply, I will never be able to talk with them in the hopes of sharing many of my own thoughts with them. I can only pray that someday a breakthrough may occur to change this. However, I must say that I have sometimes caught hopeful glimmers that convince me that strong emotions shared by dissimilar friends often do not necessarily require precise language to be successful. The emotion found in their eyes, the unique sounds that each species makes in critiquing the world, and even an exhibit of consciousness sparked by a unique sense of attitude and personality tend to project some of their strongest feelings."

Gog, having been set adrift when he lost all his ties to his own kind, knew that all friendship, whether with beast or bird, was still a bridge that was important to build. It was true, just by the nature of things, that all creatures experienced loneliness and fear; and sometimes even a gnome and the animals of the forest could give solace during these trying times—solace that was precious beyond all measure.

However, as much as Gog needed his animal friends as companions, and as much as the animals sometimes seemed to need him, their lives in general remained worlds apart. He could only live with the hope that one day a small glimmer of shared language might find its way through the chinks of existence to bridge the vast gulf between them. Until then Gog relied on Solomon, Daniel, and Rogue to fill the emptiness in his life and provide him with the vestiges of love now that they were all that were left to him.

Chapter 15
Armchair Travel

Gog was sitting in his chair, slightly rocking as he mused. He had given much thought to losing Mr. Fellows and then gaining Rogue, but it was clear that he needed some sort of pleasant diversion to take his mind off the complexities of life and those things that were so near to his heart. He often amused himself by traveling widely through time and place through reminiscing, sometimes falling into sweet, deep reverie.

On this particularly blustery March day, as the gnome daydreamed in front of the fire, he found himself skipping down a narrow forest path as a child in a time long gone by—exploring the wonders of a world that had once been totally new to him. Upon reaching a shallow creek bed, he bent over and began dredging it with a dilapidated wooden cup, searching for minnows. Dragonflies darted above his head. A muskrat following the creek in search of his own fish soon spotted Gog and quickly dove into the water to hide beneath an overhanging bank.

Gog took a wooden whistle out of his pocket. He had been trying to carve it, but the wood grain was not true; and it had split. He dropped it into the stream to see if it would float, and it did. His attention was diverted to this little boat that bobbed on the surface of the water, and then whirled in an eddy that prevented its quick passage downstream. The little gnome grinned when he caught a reflection of himself in the sunlit water. His mirrored image was eventually erased by the ripples and the retreating sun, so he diverted his attention back to his boat. His bare feet were now covered with gloriously cool mud, so he sat down on the bank and dangled them in the water to let the rushing water cleanse them. His mother would never allow him back into the house as he was.

Gog, the old gnome, now blinked; and the child was gone. He knew that he often chose to linger in his childhood because these memories were probably some of the happiest memories that he possessed. Though he occasionally also visited the older child perched upon the threshold of adulthood, reveling in the strength of the long-ago muscles and sinew that he had once used for splitting wood, tilling soil, and hiking deer trails for miles and miles—this period of his life now seemed slightly too far-fetched to him. This Gog had become almost a stranger to him as he now dealt with the aches and pains of an old man. He had to admit that he did enjoy reminiscing about the older adult that he had become years later because it was during this precious time that his mother and he had drawn even closer.

Though the mother and child ties had always been exceptionally strong, Gog and Selah had eventually become close companions and friends as both had aged. After all, they still had each other, and that was precious beyond measure. They had been able to share so much of their lives through conversation, experience, and prayer. He knew that they had both been blessed in having each other for as long as Heaven had allowed.

"Too often, when I eventually, and inevitably, revert to the old man at the end of his journey, I find myself fearing my own solitude and the threat of future death. I suppose that is why I like to keep myself busy, even when I am forced to seek my hearth. I sometimes quickly leave my chair to find solace in a cup of sweet tea or to replenish my hearth fire with wood—hoping to break my darker thoughts. I look out my solitary window, seeking to be distracted by the world beyond my cottage. Often, I decide that the time is right to bake a loaf of bread or start a fresh pot of soup. Soon my fears will be set aside by my industry, and it won't be long before Daniel and I are dozing in my rocking chair in front of the fire."

Gog wasn't sure why, but winter was often the richest time for his mind to travel; and, when it was not accompanied by dread, it allowed him to explore his inner self. It's true that during this time he was often snowbound, and his little home became both a sanctuary and a secluded island. His cottage offered him shelter from the cold and wind, but he had to remain diligent to assure that his hearth fire continued its homely glow—for himself as well as his friends. Aside from the practicalities, winter offered a slowing down of the rhythm of life, and he found comfort in this slower pace that allowed his mind time to wander.

Sometimes, he became aware of all the miracles of his own existence as he listened to his own deep breathing when he prepared for slumber, felt the pulse that throbbed within his veins, saw the plumes of steam that escaped his lips when he ventured outside, and smelled his own body and the skins of rabbits as his mittens steamed upon the hearth. With these physical rhythms of life came waves of thought that explored the hidden cavities of his mind. More questions than answers were inevitably found, but they provided rich fodder to chew on when the night seemed long and the mind remained fertile. Then Gog often found himself plumbing the very depths of thought, and it was not simple thought but thought tied to both his emotions and beliefs.

"Sometimes it seems that I can actually feel my soul flutter and beat upon my breast like a moth as it attempts to dance with flame. My soul is my very own life force.

But sometimes it seems discontent when it realizes its heavenly energy is reduced by the everyday existence found in my cottage. It seeks Light, joy, and freedom—not the constraints of winter, which is the soul's most trying season, nor the diminished space of an earthly cottage, where physical needs seem to take precedence over the spiritual. My soul is often restless. Perhaps it has been aroused by the moaning of the winter wind, the sweep of snow, or the rattle of sleet. It may be seeking answers to questions that cannot be answered, solace for the sorrows that cannot be erased, and hope for a future that is already linked to a rather troubled past."

Though Gog's soul was often not at peace during its winter confinement, he himself found a certain contentment within his home, "For these long months I am not caught up in the frantic dance of life. For a time, my life within these cottage walls is all that really matters. I can leisurely explore the world within myself without guilt or remorse for what I might be leaving undone. Time appears to stand still. The clock still chimes the passing hours, but these hours become insignificant as winter's icy breath hisses around my doorstep and the heavy snow blankets the land with white."

The mind travels were an extension of Gog's imagination, and with them he chose to be what he could not be in life: a knight wearing shining armor, a stag sporting magnificent antlers, a wild goose flying south, a limpid pool of water mirroring the sky, or a fluffy white cloud sailing high above the earth. He sometimes stretched his imagination to its limits, going places where he could not go in real life: down a woodchuck's hole, up to the moon, to the bottom of the sea, down the mystical path through the trees in his woodlands, and up to the eagle's nest that perched high above the ravine. He also dreamed about doing those things that he could not do in real life: swimming with the beavers, flying with the ravens, sitting upon a nest of goose eggs, seeing in the dark like a cat, and gathering honey as a bee.

"My mind is a wonderful vehicle for my life because it always anticipates my every wish, knowing full well that most thoughts taken from my fantasies are totally impractical; but that when I use my imagination all wishes may be explored and realized—even if it's only through mind travel and perhaps dreams. Spending my time chasing fantasy is not necessarily meaningless, for it frees me from my troubles, expands my mind to demonstrate its potential, and provides me with adventure and excitement that rivals reality."

Within this cocoon of a cottage, Gog dreamed of metamorphosis, spring, and all things new. Even within the dead of winter he caught glimpses of the many worlds beyond his, lives and places very different from his own, and times where the realities of the world were flavored with the spice of "what if."

Chapter 16
The Rites Of Spring

Along the cottage's eaves, icicles formed a row of savagely sharp teeth. Gog had been at odds with himself as to whether he should shatter them with the sweep of his broom or wait for them to gradually melt in the splendor of the thaw. He had compromised and shattered only those above his door; the rest could wait, for even now he could smell the approach of spring. An expectancy filled the air.

"Why, just yesterday, the last week in March, I came upon some pussy willows in the marsh, and they always seem to know when spring is just around the corner. Their plump, velvet coats decorate slender yellow-green twigs that, more-often-than-not, sent their roots down deep into the swamp. When I come upon them in the spring, I always feel my heart skip a beat. It is so much like finding hidden riches."

Gog had gingerly waded to a particularly healthy bush and snipped a bouquet to take back to his cottage. Though their beauty was rather homely, and they did not possess brilliant color or fragrance, still—their heralding of spring, a gentler and more pleasant season, made them precious all the same.

Over the winter Gog's cat Daniel had become sleek and sassy. The bedraggled orphan kitten was no more. He had grown in leaps and bounds, and his awkwardness as a kitten had totally disappeared, replaced by the muscles and sinew requisite for a healthy, young tom bobcat. He was now a beautiful, tawny cat, who was quite taken by himself, spending countless hours basking in the sunshine on the stoop, preening himself with countless tongue baths, and sheathing and unsheathing his sharp claws to keep them in top-notch working order.

"Vain my Daniel might be, but it's hard for me to remember a time when he was not here to provide me company. I've come to depend on my cat for his friendship. When I see him curled up upon my bed, I feel warm inside—my house feels like a home. I suppose there are some that keep a cat to rid their homes of rodents, but I keep my cat to rid my home of loneliness. What a blessing he is."

As Daniel had grown, he had become a most proficient hunter, though he continued to have a real penchant for the rabbit and partridge stews that Gog ladled from the pot on the hearth. The gnome often dined on vegetables alone, but he liked to spoil his puss; so—in deference to him he had snared a few extra rabbits and partridge over the winter months. Because of this, he now had a new feather pillow, fur-lined slippers, and a muff—items that had made the long, frigid winter easier to endure. The cat stretched to his full length on the sun-dappled stoop, and he began to sharpen his claws on the door jamb as he absorbed the heat of the sun.

Though Gog's hunting forays were essential for his survival, he had to admit that he didn't enjoy them, "If I were to find a partridge with a broken wing near my doorstep or a wounded rabbit in the forest nearby, most likely I would gently tend to the creature and eventually make a pet of it or release it back to the wild. However, If I am to survive the cruelest winters, I must set my snares so that I can gather food and insulating furs and feathers to keep me warm. Many days my teardrops fall upon my captured prey as I prepare a rabbit for stew or pluck a partridge to roast upon the spit. I have come to acknowledge the fact that life is like that. Many blessings are mixed with both joy and sorrow, and we should never accept things without realizing the sacrifices that are often made each day."

The sun's rays were still feeble, but the pattern of darkness was quickly being replaced by one of light. Even Solomon felt the coming of spring and preened his feathers and sought a bath in his shallow saucer. Though Gog knew that many setbacks with the weather were still in the making, perhaps even a snowstorm or two before flighty spring decided to stay, he chose to savor every moment as if the back of winter had been finally broken.

Spring's approach was often bittersweet for Gog, for it always flaunted new life. Woodland creatures reproduced lavish reproductions of themselves: tiny copies of fur or feathers. He looked upon these miracles in amazement. He felt a tightness around his heart and wondered what it might be like to have a mate. Most creatures had them. Reproduction was important for all species, but Gog knew little about the mysteries of family. As for the opposite sex, he had only known his mother; and that was a pure love, a lasting love, rather something divine. Taking a mate, a partner in life, would forever remain a mystery to him.

"The love for a female version of myself has never been and can never be for me. This will forever haunt me, for even gnomes have wants and wishes. My mother told me many years ago that none of my own kind exists any longer, and I must believe her.

But just the knowing never totally stops me from longing to find that something that no longer exists. I can only imagine what finding the missing piece to my own puzzle would be like. To be able to share life with another, and then to create a similar—yet uniquely new—creation through the love of both a mother and a father. A family, something that has always been no more than a myth to me. I know that all of these dreams are destined never to come true, but still—I have them, and they are bittersweet."

Once, a woodcutter had courageously wandered into Gog's lonely corner of the world, looking for straight and majestic trees for timber for a new home for himself and his family. His wife and child had accompanied him, and they had brought a picnic to share. Their child was a three-year-old daughter, a curly-topped sprite. The gnome had spied them entering his forest, and he had looked at them in wonder as he remained hidden behind a white pine. He had been entranced by the elfin beauty of the little girl who gleefully ran about the woods. Her auburn hair glistened, her pink lips pouted, and her chubby limbs danced.

The woodcutter soon decided that too many of the trees in Gog's dell were twisted and stunted and would never do for building a sturdy, durable home. He and his family, however, were delighted with their brief holiday away from their regular chores. They had relished their meager meal in the fresh air and thoroughly enjoyed each other's company. That day Gog smelled the fragrance of their pie, but he would forever go hungry. He thought back to the time when he and his own mother had tramped these very woods looking for mushrooms, wild berries, and tea roots.

"Often my mother would bring a small cast-iron pot; and we would build a small fire, using the pot to brew our tea. We would eat honey and biscuit sandwiches. We seldom tired of each other's company, for much could be spoken between us without words. We both delighted in nature's beauty and her gifts. My mother and I would test each other's observation skills, each pointing out a miracle or two that might have gone unnoticed by the other: a song sparrow's nest with speckled eggs, an empty snail shell, a fluted orange toadstool, the den of a fox, or a spider's web that glistened with dew."

"It's funny how our being together always flavored our simple meals. We munched on the same honey and biscuits that we often ate in the cottage; but out in the fresh air and sunshine with the chorus of birds and a pleasant walk beneath the towering trees—it seemed much more. The honey was sweeter, the biscuits flakier, and our time together far more precious than words can say."

Gog had watched the woodcutter and his family as they found joy in each other's company. Occasionally he caught them sharing in something that immediately reminded him of things he had once shared with his own mother. The family spread a ragged quilt upon the forest floor and proceeded to munch on bread and cheese. They shared a flask of well water to quench their thirst. Soon, the child was forced to give in to her drowsiness; and she took a brief nap with her head nestled in her mother's lap.

"The idyllic scene that I was fortunate enough to come upon in my woodland is both heartwarming and bittersweet. It reminds me of the love and caring that still take place in this old world, yet it also highlights how much I have already lost in my own life. The memories that they are now making are memories very similar to those I once made with my own mother, though our memories have already fled into my distant past."

Gog frowned in a bit of bewilderment. "I wonder what stories will be told in this family's future. They have just barely begun living their lives together, and so much yet lies before for them. I wish them well on their journey, and may their little daughter pick many wildflowers along her way."

Chapter 17
Kinship And Belonging

As Gog thought about the rich days of companionship and love when he and his mother had been a family, he was struck by what the mother and son had always avoided—talking about the future or the past. He realized with a bit of uneasiness that he and his mother had always remained comfortably in the present. They would occasionally discuss the activities they might do the next day, but that was the extent of their *future*. He thought back to those long-ago days with a bit of puzzlement, "My mother and I used to go on many rambles. Unfortunately, never once did we venture back into the past or on into the distant future in any conversation that we ever had. She made it quite clear to me that for some reason we must be satisfied for the most part with only the present, for that was all that seemed to have any consequence. I see now that in her mind all we had left to us was the present. That was our reality."

And now, after many years of solitude, Gog could appreciate why his mother had never attempted to venture beyond the *now*. For them, there had been an unspeakable past, leading only to an ongoing continuum of the present. Her legacy to her son would be that they had lived each moment fully; and, whatever the future might hold, those precious moments would be stored to compensate for whatever might come to pass—good or bad.

"The sighting of the woodcutter with his wife and daughter has stirred up a deep longing inside of me, the longing to have been able to know and love my own father. It pains me to accept the fact that I will forever lack the knowledge of who he was, what he looked like, if he had known of my existence, and why he had gone away. I will never understand why I had been so impoverished as a child, lacking in both a father and siblings. My mother was always a master of diversion and avoidance whenever I attempted to question her about our family: who they were, how my life had begun, what had taken place to destroy all traces of those like us. Perhaps truthful answers would have only caused pain. Yet, I still hunger for the knowledge of my ancestors to this very day. Because of this I will forever feel lacking."

"I know that at one time I had a father. That is the reality for all creatures. I even questioned my mother about him from time to time, but she always avoided giving me a straight-forward answer. I do know that the disappearance of my father left a void for my mother that no other could fill. I often caught Selah gazing longingly out of the window, as if she were waiting for someone—especially on balmy spring evenings. Occasionally a tear would glide down her cheek unchecked, and she would rush to hungrily enfold me in her arms as if I could ever take the place of something that had been so large."

"In an unguarded moment, my mother once told me that my father had passed away and was in heaven; but, of course, she admitted this with no details. She also told me that being a gnome could be dangerous as well as lonely, choosing not to elaborate on this information."

"Somehow, I made a connection with the loss of my father and danger; and it always filled me with sorrow. Selah once said that other beings did not always understand differences and that often fear could lead to anger. I finally surmised that one day my father had left the cottage as usual to gather kindling, but he had just never returned. My mother had remained in front of the window for days, hoping that she would eventually see him returning to our home: late, but whole and well. I'm sure that she must have dreamed of reuniting with him for many days after his disappearance. However, it was fruitless dreaming because he never did return; and my mother had to sort through her feelings and alter her realities by using her own intuition and imagination to explain his disappearance, at least to herself. Quite probably, she had never really learned what had become of the love of her life. But there were, most likely, those whom she blamed."

"I know that in all my childhood memories not one glimmer of another gnome besides my mother ever existed; and it is a fact that my father's *disappearance* occurred sometime before my third birthday. To this very day, I have never ever heard the whisper of his name. To me, my mother will always consist of sunlight and my father of shadow. I will always feel that part of myself is missing. I wish that Selah had at least talked to me about this being who had given me life so that I could at least envision him in my own mind's eye. Some sort of reality for myself might have provided me a bit of comfort, and perhaps closure."

This was the only time when Gog had mentally berated his mother for her selfishness. She had kept his father all to herself. She had never thought it necessary, or perhaps wise, to share him with her son.

"Selfish or selfless?" Gog wondered. "I will never know. Perhaps Selah was protecting me from hurtful information. That could very easily be the case. But sometimes it is easier to be angry with someone for a substantial wrong than to do battle with invisible ghosts. All thoughts of what could have been are far too pointless. My life has gone on, and now I am an *old* inhabitant of the forest who has only himself for company. I am now far older in years than my own father was when he disappeared so mysteriously. The fluctuations of time within the space of memory provide little comfort when there is no resolution."

Gog had accepted his monastic existence as best he could. He now referred to Solomon, Daniel, Rogue, and himself as *the lonely brothers*. They were together, but alone, in a world where pairs are standard, where the purpose of life is to multiply. Companionship with fellow creatures would have to provide him with the love he craved, as insufficient as it was.

"Flesh, feathers, and fur—we are an uncommon quartet of brotherhood. I can at least claim some comfort for the love we share in a dark world filled with loneliness. The sunset years of my life were never believable when I was young; and, for the most part, that is a blessing as they would have colored my every waking moment. The mystery of what might be, what can be, and what should be provides the inspiration for each new day."

Chapter 18
Finding Faith

Gog had gone on one of his rambles through the forest, rejoicing in the return of spring. He was returning home, his hat filled with snow-white mushrooms with delicate pink gills on their underbellies. He would fry some of them with the trout in his haversack and dry the rest in his rafters. A warm breeze was gently stirring the canopy of leaves above him, and he breathed in the fragrance of rain-washed sweet grasses and moss. Every so often, he pursed his lips and whistled a few notes—just because he couldn't seem to contain the joy he felt for the beauty of this day.

Gog knew that he should hurry home to clean his fish and prepare his mushrooms for his noontime meal, but he was so immersed in the pleasing landscape and the perfect weather that he took his time and savored his journey. An opening in the canopy allowed the sun to enter the clearing in which he stood and, because his face was already turning red from slightly too much exposure to the sun, Gog sidestepped back into the forest to seek the shade. Here the sunbeams made a game of playing with the shadows as they streamed light that was filled with dancing dust motes. A pattern of light and darkness fell upon the forest floor below.

In the glade, where the trees were closer together and the breezes were greatly cooled by the increase of shade, the gnome decided to stop for a moment to catch his breath before continuing. He discovered the log of an old tree that had toppled many years ago, and here he rested. He delighted in soaking up the serenity and peace of the forest. As he began to revive, his eyes explored the world of the forest around him. He saw a wild elderberry bush struggling to bud at the forest's edge, a thicket of red maple saplings unfurling their new leaves, white dogwood trees in full bloom, and a gurgling spring—still flowing ice-cold runoff from the melting snow in the distant mountains.

"My woodland home never ceases to amaze me," Gog commented. "I am never bored, mean spirited, or dissatisfied whenever I explore my own backyard. The scenery seems to change daily, and somehow the landscape always captures the emotions of any given day: whether it be sunny, rainy, blustery, or threatening storm. After a long winter, I must say that I crave the bright sunny day with scudding clouds and warm breezes. I call these days my Heaven's Gate Days, and I revel in them with all my heart and soul."

The forest floor was dappled with the sunshine that shone through the tree branches which had not yet fully leafed-out. It was mesmerizing, and he scanned it with a keen interest and delight. Gog eventually noticed that a small area over by the thicket seemed a bit out of place. While the sun-dappled forest floor seemed to sway in rhythm to the gentle breezes that whispered through the treetops, the dappled area in front of the thicket remained stationary. He wandered over to the stand of saplings to investigate this strange occurrence.

As Gog's eyes focused on the ground in the thicket, he soon began to grin. The mystery had been solved. A small spotted fawn, brilliantly camouflaged to match her surroundings, lay nestled on the ground. Gog walked closer to the little deer and was surprised when the creature showed absolutely no acknowledgment of his presence. Baffled, his curiosity soon outweighed his normal reaction, which was to avoid all wildlife as quickly as he found them. However, in this case, something just didn't seem right; and he decided to determine if there was something wrong with the little deer.

Because the fawn was so still, and continued to totally ignore his presence, Gog began to fear that perhaps she was dead. He gently whispered to the little doe—hoping not to startle her, but to make sure that she was only sleeping, "Little one, are you okay? I don't mean to disturb your slumber. You look so peaceful, but I just want to make sure that everything is okay."

The fawn quickly raised her tiny head, and her eyelids slowly fluttered open to reveal two eyes—eyes that were covered with an opaque white film, eyes that lacked the ability to focus on anything in front of her. Gog could not believe his own eyes, especially when he soon came to the realization that the seemingly-perfect little woodland creature bedded down before him was—blind. He gasped in distress! He then carefully backed away and returned to his seat on the fallen tree.

"The little fawn cannot be more than a day old, and yet she has come into this world without sight. How will she ever survive living in the forest without the ability to see where she is going. God above must have plans for her, yet I cannot see how these plans will ever allow her the kind of life she deserves."

Gog glanced over at the little fawn, who had quickly returned to her slumbers. "How will this little deer ever navigate the forest without her sight? She will need to be swift on her feet to escape her enemies, quick to follow her mother and the herd, and agile enough to navigate a landscape that is filled with obstacles. My heart leaps in my chest as I consider her trying to do all these things as a blind deer. I fear for her very survival."

The good-hearted gnome sat there for a while, pondering the fate of the sweet little creature he had just discovered in his woods.

And then he began to think about the possibility of trying to save her.

"The little doe is the tiniest of bundles. Perhaps I could carry her back to my cottage where I could take the responsibility of caring for her myself. Most certainly she will take up very little space by my hearth, at least until she grows to any size. I could fashion a woven collar with a tether so that I could lead her out into the woods to graze during the day and then bring her back into my home for protection at night. Once she grows to full size, I could tether my little deer next to my summer kitchen where I could keep her supplied with water and food. I would give her constant care and attention, trying my very best to make up for her lack of sight."

Gog's rosy picture of saving the little fawn soon began to fade as he became more practical in his assessment of the situation. "My little fawn is newly-born, and she is still nursing. She needs her mother's milk to grow strong and healthy. She also needs her mother. I cannot even begin to think of taking her away from the one who loves her the most and cares for her to the best of her ability. This little deer is not like my Daniel, who had lost ties with family and been truly abandoned. I must never forget that Daniel chose to live with me. I allowed him freedom of choice. Even at this very moment, if he decided to amble away from the cottage, never to return, there is nothing to stop him from doing so."

"Solomon, my little crippled chickadee, lives in a cage—that much is true. But, without a doubt, the cage is necessary for his very existence. It is a safe home of sorts where he can live a full life with my friendship and plenty of food and drink. He could never survive without my help. He lost the freedom of choice, but he has been given a means to continue his life with friendship and without want. His only other option would have been death."

A fawn, however, needs to gambol about the forest—browsing on bushes and grass, munching acorns, and quenching her thirst in a nearby stream. She will rely on naps beneath the shade of a tree—often nestling with a mother, a brother or sister, and perhaps a sprinkling of aunts. And, though she is blind, perhaps her life might very well continue with most of these deer activities What can I offer this little one but myself—which might include safety but would never alone be enough for her happiness."

"I suppose that if I had found her as an orphan that my concern for her might be more realistic. Perhaps it might then be a matter of life and death, and I would have more right on my side. But I know in my heart that this tiny blind fawn has a mother somewhere nearby who is just waiting for me to leave so that she may rejoin her tiny daughter. She will return to the fawn with her mother's milk, a mother's care, and a mother's love. Blind her baby may be, but she still possesses so much. I must not even consider taking her away from all that she has. Her fate has been determined by her Maker, and I know that I must not interfere. She was born wild, and wild she must remain."

The gnome eventually trudged on home, still a bit heart-broken about the possible fate of the little fawn that he had already come to love.

***

Gog chose to leave the fawn as he had found her, but he had still gone back to his cottage with his brows knit in worry and concern for this most vulnerable of creatures who had been born into the world with a terrible disadvantage. But God had decreed a life's path for the little fawn, and Gog had to abide by his Maker's decision. He had placed her fate in God's hands where it belonged. She would be raised by her mother and the herd to the best of their ability. And, though her destiny was uncertain, what would be would be.

"I made my decision not to interfere, and I am convinced it was the right one. I was not meant to contradict Heaven's wishes. Still, I continue to worry about her. The little doe has found a way into my heart, and I have come to think of her as Faith. I think of her often, wondering how she is faring with her blindness, if her mother is successful in helping her to compensate for not having sight, and if she is being treated kindly by the rest of the herd."

Time went by, and eventually Gog was given the golden opportunity to see for himself how the little fawn who had captured his heart was faring.

"I happened upon Faith one day when I went to the stream for water. She was close by her mother and, though she was perhaps a bit more hesitant than others her age, it was almost impossible to tell that she was lacking in sight. Her white spots were beginning to fade, and her burnished coat was turning to a sweet summer brown. She looked content, and it was very clear that she was where she belonged. I cannot tell you how this sighting lifted my spirits."

While Gog watched the herd from the midst of a thicket, he noticed that the little deer remained close to her mother's side. She now stood on sturdy legs, delicately nibbling newly emerging leaves from the underbrush as her mother remained in an attitude of rest. It was very clear that Faith was part of a very close family. Another large doe lay next to Faith's mother, and this doe was a mother to a newborn fawn—small and spotted—lying by her side. An adolescent buck stood alert, hidden in the deeper shadows of the woods. It appeared that he was positioned to keep guard over the little herd. Gog's spirits lifted as he realized that Faith was right where she was supposed to be—with her family.

***

Gog became caught up in his numerous summer chores, ultimately preparing for the hard winter ahead, which would become a reality in a few months. He occasionally thought of Faith with fondness, wondering if she was able to succeed in the wild. He always kept a sharp eye out for her, in the hopes of seeing her once again.

The harvest had been brought in, the wood had been cut and stacked, and many beeswax candles had been dipped. Winter was just around the corner. On a beautiful Indian Summer day, when the cobalt blue skies were mirrored in the pool and the last of the orange leaves were floating to earth, Gog took his haversack and took a path that meandered deep into the forest. He wanted to scout the land for possible *treasure*, enjoying a precious day that still held summer's rays as it continued to ignore the possibility of a killing frost.

On his way home from his wanderings, Gog had decided that he would fill his empty haversack with butternuts. They were now ripe, and many lay scattered upon the carpet of moss beneath the butternut tree. Just as Gog bent down to pick up a handful of nuts, he caught a flash of white out of the corner of his eye. He quickly stood up, and it was then that he spied Faith—a half-grown deer now who only slightly resembled the little fawn he had first seen in the thicket. Still, he knew her. His eyes and his heart easily recognized her.

"My Faith has grown into a beautiful doe. She is not timid or hesitant, and she is very much a part of the herd. When I pick up the butternuts, every deer's head quickly rises in a bit of panic—except Faith's. I truly think she still recognizes me. The lead deer finally decides that it is time for the herd to depart, and they do so in haste. They quickly skirt the dense brush, charge between trees with little if any room to spare, and easily leap over logs and debris that are in their way. And my little Faith is as fast and nimble as any of them. I am totally amazed!"

"I wonder how Faith has been able to conquer her blindness. Surely there has been no miracle to erase it. Yet, as I watch her leave, I notice an alertness that far surpasses that of her fellow deer. Her head is held a bit higher to heighten her hearing and when she briefly touches her mother who is running just ahead of her, she quickly corrects her course. I believe that Faith has probably recognized my smell, even at such a distance, and knows that she has little to fear of me. Though she has never possessed sight, she can most certainly smell, touch, taste, and hear. These senses may very well have become magnified to compensate for her loss of sight."

"The little blind fawn that I once found in my forest is growing into a magnificent doe. I will go to bed this night without a worry for her well-being. She has become part of a family, part of the forest, and part of all nature. Blessings to her and thanksgiving to my God in Heaven."

***

Time went by, and twice the procession of seasons passed. On a lovely spring morn, Gog happened upon twin spotted fawns lying close by one another in the very same protective thicket where he had once found Faith. He just knew without a bit of doubt to whom these offspring belonged—his forest friend Faith. He also knew with all his heart that we must be very close by, for he could sense her presence. However, being true to her wild nature now, she did not show herself—continuing to watch him from a distance. And her little fawns, cuddled together on the sun-dappled forest floor, did not move a muscle. They were very still and very quiet, hoping to go unnoticed by those that might harm them. They quietly and patiently waited for their mother to return.

"Faith, my little blind deer, has certainly done herself proud, truly making a life for herself despite her loss of sight. I am so overjoyed that she now has a family of her own! Whether or not I will ever see her again is no longer my concern. I know that she has succeeded in life, and I am content with that."

Gog slung his haversack over his shoulder. This day it was filled with dandelion greens and wild onions. He followed a mossy path that meandered away from the fawns but would eventually lead him home. His footsteps were careful and rather soft, for he did not want to disturb the gentle sleep of Faith's fawns. His heart sang with joy.

Chapter 19
A Glow In The Glade

Gog's memories of his mother and their life together continued to both haunt him and comfort him as time went by. He cherished what they had once been able to share as mother and son. He fondly remembered one evening in the middle of summer when Selah and he planned a bonfire to celebrate their journey of life. It was Summer Solstice. Selah had baked a wild strawberry tart and had steeped a pot of tea for their refreshments for this special event. They had just finished their festive repast and were huddled beneath her shawl to stave off the cool, sitting next to the bonfire where its smoke could repel the hungry mosquitoes.

As they sat there trading stories and observations, Gog saw a brief flash of light deep in the glen. Suddenly, another brief twinkling glowed in the short distance before him; but then it seemed to be immediately snuffed out—almost as quickly as it had first appeared, blinking on in a brief beacon of light. Gog thrust off the shawl that was covering him and stood up in excitement. He stood hesitantly waiting, not knowing when or where the next mysterious light might occur.

"Mother, what was that?" Gog asked in anticipation. He peered into the depths of the forest, and to his amazement more lights began to glow, twinkling on and off in a merry display of sporadic light. The invisible light bearers were weaving their way beneath the canopy of the many oaks and maples in the dell. The show was mesmerizing and delightful.

"Why, son, those are lightning bugs. Surely, you remember them from last summer. Every summer these little insects come together to greet one another, and they glow in the glade as an expression of their delight in meeting once again. Their light display is a way for them to communicate."

"Could I catch one, Mother? Or even two? Perhaps three? Maybe I could put them in a jar so that they could light our way back home. Maybe we could use them to light our cottage in the evening when it is too hot and muggy for candles. They are so beautiful! There must be a way to make their wonderful light last for more than just a moment."

Gog had been enthralled by the light show that was on display in the woods. The twinkling lights of the tiny insects were emphasized by the magical backdrop behind the trees in the foreground that stood in dark, stark contrast to them.

The little gnome ran out to the edge of the woods and attempted to find a lightning bug so that he could study it and then perhaps catch it, but he soon found them to be far too elusive. Just as he located one, it would turn off its light; and he would be sidetracked by another that seemed even closer and brighter. They appeared to be very easy to catch, but they were not. Pursuing them caused nothing but total frustration for Gog, and he soon realized that their magic and beauty were far more potent when viewed from a distance. His mother's tinkling laughter finally brought him back to her side, and when he sat down his face mirrored his disappointment. Selah draped her arms around her child's shoulders in sympathy. She could sense his sadness at this turn of events.

"Gog, sometimes we mortals must accept the magic that is gifted to us by our Maker as just that—magic. We should appreciate the beauty of it, enjoy it for as long as it lasts, and be delighted that we have been chosen to experience it. Many things in nature can't, and shouldn't be, *captured.* No creature wants to be owned and controlled by another. Certainly, you would never have found happiness if an ogre had taken possession of you."

Gog's mother had told him countless bedtime stories where the ugly, evil ogre was a threat in the storybook world. He had envisioned this monster in his mind numerous times, and he had always been in awe of its awfulness. The little gnome quickly looked at his mother with fear in his eyes.

"Mother, that would be dreadful. If I had been caught by an ogre, I might have been eaten. Or if he thought that I was too tough for his supper, he might have kept me out of spite. I would never see you again, and my heart would be broken. I would miss my home and my woodland friends and my own little bed." He wrapped a fold of the shawl closer around his shoulders as if to protect himself from the dangers that he now imagined lurking in the night.

His mother nodded and then swept him further into her embrace. "You understand well, my son. All creatures have families and homes and wish to be free.

Though we must sometimes depend on the sacrifice of special animals for our daily lives, such as the rabbit and the partridge, to capture them or others only for selfish pleasure is wrong. When we try to impose our will on them, it is against what we would want for ourselves."

She went on, "We would never wish to play the part of the ogre and rob others of their homes and family. I look out into the darkness of the glade, and I imagine that the world has burst forth with fairies that are carrying twinkling stars from shrub to shrub in a joyful summer dance. I can't imagine choosing to spoil their fun by intruding on their sport."

"I surely see the twinkling stars, Mother. I think you must be right! The fairies are very nimble and smart; and I'm sure that the stars help light their way, so they don't stumble when they dance. I most certainly don't want to do anything to spoil their fun."

Selah smiled. "Your imagination can see many things, Gog. Appreciating the goodness in magic may help us to imagine a world colored with love and joy. Being able to imagine how another creature thinks or feels is a way for us to understand and acknowledge them."

The mother and child finished their steaming cups of tea by the fire, and soon the Gog child fell blissfully asleep, peaceful in his slumber.

***

Gog blinked as he came out of his reverie. Though he was reluctant to leave the mind wanderings of his past, he knew he must. As pleasant as those days had been, they had also come to an end. He knew that the memories he had accumulated were precious; but, unfortunately, they were just that—memories. They were not real or substantial, and they were never meant to last. Like the first snowflake, they soon melted and disappeared.

"It's amazing how so many years have gone by as quickly as they have! How easy it is to bring these memories back, at least for a moment. But often there is a sense of sadness attached to them because now they are nothing more than illusions. The precious moments we once shared can never be truly relived. It is hard to realize that sometimes the most cherished memories can often be painful, even more painful than those filled with sorrow or disaster. We may be able to avoid memories that were painful, choosing not to revisit them; but the cherished memories leave us thirsting for them again and again—for, incredibly, we wish to relive them.

Knowing that they can only happen in a dream, and that quite often they might bring about a sense of pain and loss as well, we still seek to revisit them."

Chapter 20
The Cost Of Survival

Gog had spent a very long day in his garden hoeing between the rows, weeding amongst the plants, fertilizing and watering, and finally mulching. He had quickly washed up in the cold-water spring, and then he returned home where he eased himself down upon the stoop in his backyard to rest his weary bones. He removed his hat and leaned back upon the half-opened door of the cottage to rest. The door was soon deemed far too uncomfortable, so he made a makeshift pillow with his haversack. Soon he was sound asleep.

The balmy June afternoon was on the wane, and Gog eventually awakened to the drone of the flies and the quiet hush that only came as daylight began to come to an end.

Recovering from his drowsy state, Gog looked around and noticed the lengthening shadows.

A sprouting acorn, captured in a final ray of sun, basked for one last moment. A chipmunk with its cheeks bulging with the brothers and sisters of this fledgling new tree scurried by, hoping to gain his hidden home before some hungry owl took to the woods in search of prey. The chipmunk, finding room in his cheeks for just one more treasure, snatched up the sprouting acorn and quickly departed.

In a dreamlike stupor, the gnome stood up, grabbed his hat, and pushed the back door open. He entered his cottage and smiled at the aroma of the vegetable soup in the cauldron. He had worked very hard this day and was famished. Gog saw Solomon peering at him through his willow cage; and Daniel the bobcat was stretched out upon the rug in front of the hearth, luxuriating in the last red-hot embers in the fireplace that were keeping the soup warm.

Though the cat had recently eased his hunger by feasting on a mouse and a tender bird, he certainly looked the picture of peace and innocence. The killer that crouched within him was once again costumed in furs and purrs. When he saw Gog approach, he slowly stood and stretched, arching his back for the inevitable stroking he had come to expect. Daniel could not really be accused of being evil because he was a prime example of the survival instinct that existed in nature.

In nature, everything had a purpose. Animals needed to follow their instincts just to live, so it was not fair to judge them either good or bad. The rules were very complicated. Their lives depended on this thing called *survival*, this extremely strong will to live by any means possible. Killing others was the only method available to predatory birds and animals for guaranteeing their food for the day, and getting food was necessary just for them to live. Gog sometimes tried to understand why all this killing was necessary, at the same time admitting his own guilt in obtaining the meat and hide of some animals for his own survival. He realized that it was all very confusing, and sometimes impossible to fully understand.

Gog wondered why some creatures were selected to be the predators who did the killing while others were designated as the prey and had been chosen to be the ones killed and eaten. But he quickly realized that it wasn't even as simple as that because some predators often became prey for other predators. It was all so confusing. There were so many times when Gog puzzled over his own responsibility in the various roles he played as he himself continued to strive to live.

"If one chooses to protect the innocent from becoming prey, where does one begin? Snatching a rabbit from a hawk? A mouse from a weasel? A butterfly from a wren? A beetle from a praying mantis? To survive we are all programmed by our Maker to do what we must do to live this life we have been given. In this world it seems that balances are always sought: a balance of life and death, of pleasure and pain, of gain and loss. Sometimes things just are, and even though we may find it hard to accept, it really is far beyond our control. Being merciful and thankful for the success of the hunt. . . now that is what seems to separate us from our wild brothers and sisters. Unfortunately, they have not come equipped to understand the concept of *blessings* in this world in which we live."

Daniel was indeed dense, to the point of being downright ignorant, when it came to how he regarded his own prey. This self-absorbed cat who sat upon the stoop had concerns mostly for his own gnawing hunger pains, and he sought to take care of them the only way he knew how—by hunting his prey. He was also playful and fun-loving, and he chose to spend far too much time tormenting his prey before he finally settled down to eating it. This was an enjoyable pastime for Daniel, but—most definitely not—for his prey. The cat, unfortunately, was not privy to the teachings of **The Good Book**; and he had never learned to *do unto others as you would have them do unto you.* But he was one of God's creatures, and he followed his Maker's prescription for his own life.

He was clearly a creature created by God, who instinctually followed God's dictates of what it is to be a bobcat, a wild animal who is part of a natural world. He was programmed to behave in a specific way, and he did. But Daniel had also become a fireside cat who had a human keeper, so his instincts had been necessarily diluted—to a point. Now, he could also play the part of a rather lovable creature, sitting upon Gog's lap for hours—purring and twitching his tail. But he always remained alert for the tiny scuttle of feet: a mouse for dinner or for a toy—for he was, after all, an opportunist.

As a cousin of man, Gog thought about this battle for survival and how thinking about doing and just doing without thinking could sometimes be in conflict. Animals in the wild followed their instinct and their actions pertaining to the hunt were immediate and swift. On the other hand, even a lowly woodland gnome took the time to question the rightness of participating in the hunt, even if survival was dependent upon it. Gog knew that there were no rights or wrongs in this issue, for in the end survival was essential to all.

Gog tried to argue his own feelings on this, "I have been created by my Maker, and the rules I follow are for the most part pre-ordained. There are many different types of hunger, however, and it has been necessary for me to try to distinguish between them over the course of my lifetime. With all my needs I must also learn to recognize the existence of good and evil, and what I should and should not hunger for."

Gog filled a bowl with vegetable soup and then sat down to sup. The night was starting to close in, so he lit the stub of a candle and watched it flicker for a moment.

This little bit of light was enough to chase away some of the lurking shadows; and the fireplace continued to cast a radiant glow upon the hearth. Together they provided just enough light for the inhabitants of the cottage.

"Survival for me is a very complicated proposition. I hunt a few animals and birds to sustain the demands of my cooking pot, and I gather materials that will protect the heat within my body from the dreaded cold over the winter months. These animals are not my enemies; but, unfortunately, my needs require their sacrifice so that I may continue my own life. Because of their sacrifice, it is important for me to be humble about their loss of life and to be very, very grateful for their existence. I must count my blessings in their regards."

"All living creatures are dependent on others for their lives, whether knowingly or unknowingly. As we live our lives, we soon learn that we must accept the commands of this world in which we find ourselves. We come to realize that there are spiritual laws that help us to be good, and there are also natural laws which help us to survive. Both laws are derived from God, and we have little choice but to follow them."

Gog knew that he would never totally be able to accept the many deaths that were necessary to sustain the many other lives in the woods. He was far too soft-hearted. Daniel, as predator, was a prime example of that; and, necessarily, so was he. But the food chain that existed in the natural world where each insect, bird, or animal was either the predator or the prey—and sometimes both, was the prime example of how natural laws eventually ruled over those made by man. Perhaps mankind would never totally understand nature's workings, but one day it might certainly learn to appreciate them.

"Whether or not I eat rabbit stew is really not the point," Gog decided. "I am following a destiny laid out for me by my Maker. What is important is that I always appreciate the sacrifices that are made, that killing is never a pleasant occupation that is ever done unnecessarily, and that when I feel it is necessary to kill that I give both God and my prey thanks for the blessings of each meal that is set before me."

Gog began to eat his vegetable soup with relish. He gave a bowl of broth to Daniel and sprinkled a few sunflower seeds in Solomon's cage for his evening meal. The long day was winding down. Gog replenished his hearth with firewood, and the voracious flames were soon licking their way up the chimney, snapping and crackling as they went. He pulled his chair a bit closer to his hearth, poured himself a small glass of dandelion wine, and then placed Daniel upon his lap. Soon he was nodding off to sleep in front of the fire, enjoying the warmth and comfort of his little home.

Chapter 21
Martha The Chipmunk

One day when Gog was sitting upon his stoop, cleaning his mud-caked shoes before entering his cottage, he noticed that a brand-new hole had been dug to the right of the wild apple tree in his backyard. A mound of unearthed pebbles and soil ringed this new hole, and sporadically a fresh shower of earth could be seen spurting up into the air. It was clear that an excavation of some sort was currently underway. A little chipmunk eventually poked her head up through the new hole, surveyed the location of her new summer home, and then saucily chirped at Gog. She had taken possession of this plot of land and now deemed him to be a troublesome trespasser. Then she disappeared for a time, evidently attending to the many duties that came with establishing this new home.

Gog was fascinated by the little chipmunk's unexpected arrival, and he sat on his stoop overlong now, hoping to catch a glimpse of this elusive new neighbor. "I've already named my tiny friend Martha because of her industry and because it seems to fit her pert, very outgoing personality— a personality far larger than her miniature self. She appears to be a very intense little chipmunk, and she seems not to be overshadowed by those who are bigger and fiercer."

Days passed, and it was clear that Martha was here to stay. The industrious little chipmunk soon completed her underground home, and she could be seen—cheeks bulging—carrying foodstuffs down her hole from dawn to dusk. She never paused, it seemed, not even to take in the scenery or to indulge in a personal grooming session. She was intent upon increasing her stores for the winter, hoping that her industry would guarantee her sustenance through the long winter months.

Gog, the provider, was quick to leave handouts for his new visitor. His friendly nature always encouraged him to offer hospitality to any new acquaintance. He thoroughly enjoyed his role as a host and received much joy in sharing his foodstuffs with those who might enjoy them and benefit by them.

"I leave Martha a few tidbits on my stoop—an acorn, a few blackberries, a crust of bread—hoping to entice her closer. I would like to think that she sees these gifts as a sign of welcome. Food at most is viewed as an open invitation to friendship, and at least as a token of good will. I will watch and wait, hoping to catch her reaction as she discovers this new bounty."

Martha eventually appeared, scurried over to the mysterious picnic, and rapidly filled her cheeks with the unexpected plunder. She didn't take the time to sample any of these goodies because she was far more intent upon securing them for future use. She quickly dashed back to her underground home, so she could stash them away. The chipmunk was still very wary of her new surroundings, and the creature that seemed rather overly anxious to befriend her made her very nervous.

As time passed, however, Martha became very used to the handouts that Gog set out for her—to the point where she came to expect them and rely upon them. She also learned to become comfortable in his presence. She no longer feared him and didn't even trouble herself to avoid him. In fact, one day when Gog had forgotten to leave Martha her daily rations, she let him know with plaintive, angry cheeps. She was impatient with herself for coming to rely on this two-legged creature and incensed with his lack of dependability. She had come to rely on these provident hand-outs, but her cheeks were now empty when she had counted on his continued good will in helping her to keep them filled.

Exasperated, she cheeped to anyone who would listen. *This creature that walks on two legs has decided to shadow my front door continually. Not only that, but for reasons I do not understand—he leaves me enough food, good food and interesting food, so that what I gather elsewhere for myself may be stored for future use. I certainly don't wish to dip into my food savings for my daily meals if I don't have to. The cold season is coming, that I know. I can't afford to eat my own stashed supply this early in the season if I do not have to. But some days, when I arrive to gather my day's dinner—which has usually shown up on a regular basis—I find an empty plate! I just cannot manage with this inconsistency!*

Becoming bolder and bolder as she became more closely acquainted with Gog's habits and movements, Martha's constant demands for food became almost comical. Gog began to exploit her impatience by personally doling out her food. "I tempt her to come closer to retrieve her treats by hiding her tidbits on my person rather than on the doorstep. I place tasty bits of food between my fingertips and toes, a bended elbow, or an open pocket on my shirt. Then I take care to resemble a statue, even monitoring the breaths I take so that I won't startle her by my movement."

Gog's ploy began to work, and soon Martha was scurrying up and down his legs, across an arm, and around his neck in search of treats. He always smiled as she scampered about his body, but he never moved a muscle. This game that he had taught her was proving to be highly entertaining!

"It seems that little Martha is almost always very hungry and anxious to retrieve something for her cheeks. She cannot resist the sights and smells of some of her favorite foods. Soon she is taking tidbits from every location where they are hidden upon my person. She cheeps away saucily while she is scurrying up and down my body's frame to retrieve her treats. Sometimes I can't help myself, and she makes me laugh aloud—a full-bellied chuckle. Then she will retreat for a moment in disgust because my laughter has interrupted the serious business of her food-gathering."

When exasperated by Gog's conduct, Martha sometimes sat upon the ground in front of him and stewed. He was both a mystery to her, as well as a bother. But she never forgot to remind herself that he was also her benefactor. So, on this note, her dissatisfaction with Gog never lasted but a moment or two because the little chipmunk really did think that she had the gnome all figured out.

I am no longer intimidated by this creature's presence. When he happens upon the scene each day, I can quickly see the locations of all the hidden treats. He has become very predictable in where he hides them, so I always hurry to retrieve them. I no longer fear him, so it doesn't matter to me if my dinner is to be found on the ground by his feet or on his person. I quickly gather what he has laid out for me and then scamper home with it safely tucked in my cheeks. I amaze myself at what I will do for a few tidbits for my winter pantry!

Gog was besotted with his little guest, and each day was more than a little brighter because of her presence. He knew that his delight stemmed in part from her very entertaining personality and her determination. It was hard to remember what his life had been like prior to her entrance a few weeks past. He grinned as he envisioned her and the various escapades that they had shared.

"My Martha is a rather tiny little female. Her coat is not quite so brilliantly chestnut as some chipmunks I have seen, and her tail is not quite as long and bushy as others. But she is certainly sassy and clever, and sometimes she exhibits the sweetest of dispositions. Oh, she can be saucy and determined at times—that is certainly true. But, I must admit that I sometimes feel a bit of gentle consideration for me on her part; and, my oh my, she adds so much gaiety and light to my existence!"

Sometimes, after the little chipmunk had stashed all her tidbits in her hole; she came back and perched upon Gog's lap to chitter away. Gog would cock his head and listen intently but, try as he might, he could never understand any of her chipmunk language. Still, she amused him by keeping him company, and she was faithful in making her daily visits. Gog often thought about these new ties that bound him to his little friend.

"I know that most of my animal friends are attached to me by the ties of hunger and need. They love what I give them more than they love me for who I am. I am realistic about that. I know that these creatures are by nature mostly just out to survive. They are wary of others, but highly motivated to fill their bellies whenever given the opportunity. Yet, I can never totally discount the possibility that Martha might also feel glimmers of love and friendship towards me as well, warm feelings that I certainly have for her. I know that she enriches my existence and fills a void in my life with a joy that tempers some of life's harshest heartaches." He watched Martha as she scurried back to her den with a piece of dried apple, and he couldn't help but smile.

***

At the end of summer, Martha disappeared. Gog had had dark premonitions that this would probably be the case one day. However, he continued to watch for her—hoping that he would be proven wrong. However, he remained constantly disappointed by her continuing absence. Two days went by, and then three, and finally four. He hoped against hope that her disappearance might have stemmed from a natural occurrence that was quite likely for any woodland creature. Perhaps the little chipmunk had finally found a mate, gone off to establish a more convenient winter home, or tired of his company. However, deep down inside Gog knew that he was only fooling himself.

"I have begun to fear that Martha's disappearance might be based on something far more troubling—perhaps even sinister in a way. I am reminded in so many ways of Mr. Fellows' disappearance. There are so many things in the natural world that present danger, and many of them could have caused her demise. I can't help but think that

Rogue the fox and Daniel the cat might be prime suspects in the little chipmunk's disappearance, for they must be constantly vigilant to attain their next meal. I certainly hope I am wrong, and that neither of them has betrayed me by dining on my little friend. But it is a possibility, and I must be realistic about this life in which I live."

Gog knew in his heart-of-hearts that Rogue and Daniel could not be blamed for having made a meal of Martha, if this did indeed prove to be the case, for they were but living out their natural lives based on instinct and survival. Still, he felt a certain shifting of his loyalties. He grieved for the little lost soul of Martha and for the death of his own innocence that now led him to believe that one of his closest friends might very well be the culprit who had taken the life of one whom he held dear. Being rational was one thing, but sorely grieving over loss was another.

"I know that I have no proof that either friend has been responsible for Martha's disappearance, and that many other woodland inhabitants might very well have seen to her death—if she has indeed been taken that way. Yet I am still troubled by the possibility that my friends the fox or the bobcat may be to blame. And I do so miss her! She was the light in my day, and I had come to depend on her sunny disposition for so much of my happiness."

Sadly, Martha's disappearance was permanent, and Gog never did see her again. He eventually forgave Rogue and Daniel, just on principal, for had one of them been the actual culprit—he had done what had been prescribed for him by his Maker. Gog was powerless to change the laws of nature made by God's decree, regardless of the pain and suffering he might have to withstand because of it.

"All things in life have a purpose and, just because the purpose is sometimes hard to understand, I must learn to accept life as it comes. This is a hard lesson. Rogue continues to follow discreetly at my heels, and Daniel continues to curl up on my lap as evening descends. Yet, I continue to grieve for my little Martha who was snatched from my life before we even had a chance to become thoroughly acquainted. Though I sorely do miss her, I will always remember her with fondness."

Gog was only just beginning to accept that tragedy was an integral part of life. Though he was still reeling from the loss of Mr. Fellows, which he had deemed as senseless, he now had to face his grief over the loss of Martha. He knew that he should not be surprised or overly-saddened, for death was but a part of life. God had a plan for all living things, and his Savior was there to guide him along the way. He knew that he could not rejoice over new life—a hatch of goslings, a birth of a fawn, or a nest of baby wrens—without the realization that death was also going to be doled out in equal measure. But he also knew that soft hearts filled with love necessarily grieved over the loss of those who departed this world before them, and he knew that he was no exception.

“I sometimes think that my life is a patchwork of memories and feelings for those I have come to love. All my joys and sorrows provide me with the road markers for my own life. I may not know exactly where I am going from year to year, but these milestones will remind me of where I have been. Joy and sadness will continue as my fellow travelers for as long as I live upon this earth.”

“I know that our personalities and characters are gradually formed over time just as raw clay eventually comes to life in the form of a statue or a bowl. Some of us may crack in the unforgiving kiln of life while others take on a fine color and patina magnificent to behold. I would like to think that something positive, meaningful, and perhaps even beautiful might be born from tragic circumstance as well as joyous occasion. Unfortunately, I am not sure that I will always fully accept the importance of grief in our lives. It is too heart-rending to think that death must share the precious stage of life with birth. I do know that for my own sake I need to always forgive, forget, and bear witness to hope. But more powerful than all that: “Thy will be done on earth as it is in Heaven.”

Chapter 22
A Storm's Fury

The air in the dale hung heavy and humid, and not even the semblance of a breeze penetrated the woodlands. Gog sat upon his stoop, lethargic with the heat, snapping beans for his evening meal. Daniel was perched next to him, lackadaisically licking his fur as he attended to a hit-or-miss tongue bath which he had little passion for. He too was exhausted from the heat. Rogue could be seen in the distance, curled up in a nest of pine needles in the deep shade by the brook. The fox in his afternoon slumber seemed to blend into the indistinct shadows, making him close to invisible.

Storm clouds were beginning to roll in, and the static electricity in the air set nerves tingling and shivers skating up and down the spine. A brilliant flash of lightning lit up the sky, and though Gog knew that it was still miles away—the following crash of thunder was both powerful and ominous. The rumble was a warning for those who had not already sought shelter to do so at once.

Rogue immediately jumped up and glided like a ghost into his nearby den. Daniel padded back into the cottage, leaped up on the bed, and curled into the quilt—using comfort as his defense mechanism. And Gog quickly picked up his pot of beans and hurried inside so that he could hang them on the tripod over the coals to simmer, so they would be ready for his supper once the storm passed by. He then made sure that the latch on the backdoor was fast. Glancing at the diminishing fire, he decided he would let it go out. He did not want to take the risk of encouraging heavy gusts of wind from the approaching storm to whistle down his chimney, scattering embers and huffing smoke throughout his cottage. Gog could hear the wind moan outside as it increased in strength and volatility.

The wind continued to pick up until it was tossing the branches helter-skelter. Its howl was soon overwhelmed by a deluge of slanting rain that drummed upon the cottage's roof, beat upon the window, and quickly erased what little remained of the daylight. An ominous yellow light peered in the one window until it was quickly doused by the darkening atmosphere that surrounded the cottage.

The force of the storm was not going to diminish anytime soon. Gog could tell. As the rain picked up in volume, so too did the ferocity of the wind. Soon the very forest floor shook with the cloud-to-ground lightning that was crashing all around. A loud boom of thunder echoed throughout the wooded glen and struck terror in the hearts of those forced to listen to this violent concert that was showcasing the clashing of cymbals and the beating of drums.

The few remaining red coals in the fireplace began to send out puffs of smoke from the downdrafts that raced down the chimney. Gog and Daniel soon hid beneath the quilt on the bed, refusing to stir until nature's temper tantrum decided to come to an end. Every time an especially large clap of thunder shook the cottage, the gnome and cat jumped in nervousness and then shook with fear.

Solomon had made an impromptu nest in the corner of his willow cage, using bits and pieces of refuse, twigs, and feathers. Here he hunkered down with his black-capped head frozen beneath his wing. He ruffled his feathers to insulate his chilled body, shivering from the unseasonably cool temperature that had plunged downwards with the onslaught of icy rain. Not once did he chirp out his displeasure but, instead, fearfully trembled in his cage—waiting for the storm to wear itself out.

The storm continued for what seemed like hours, but eventually its strength began to gradually diminish. Just as the inhabitants of the cottage were beginning to breathe a sigh of relief, counting on the lessening of the rain, wind, and thunder as proof that the storm was reaching its conclusion, a ferocious crack of lightning, followed by what seemed to be an explosion and a violent shaking of the earth, totally lit up the sky. Shortly afterwards, another ominous, though lesser crash of thunder, indicated just how close-by the encounter had been.

This loud, most violent of crashes reverberated from less than a mile away. Cloyingly pungent fumes of sulfur and wood smoke mysteriously filtered through the forest. The fumes seemed to originate from the storm's nearby lightning strike, damage site of where it had wreaked its latest violence—site unknown. The foul-smelling fog was having difficulty in rising heavenward from the location of the strike, and it skirted the woodlands with ghostly fingers that raked through the undergrowth and filtered through the branches of the trees. Weak flickers of flame could be seen at a distance where the ferocious lightning had come to earth and struck an unsuspecting target, but the festering flames were quickly being doused by the drumming rain.

Gog sat up in his bed and threw his blankets aside. He still cradled Daniel in his arms for comfort and trembled with fear, thinking that the world had very possibly gone mad just outside his door. He knew that he had never experienced anything so wild as this recent display of nature's tempestuousness ever before, and he hoped he never would again.

"When I heard the tremendous crash, it seemed that my heart immediately stopped. I know that something ominous has taken place, and I can't even begin to imagine what it might be. After whispering many fervent prayers to my God above, I know that it is now time to face whatever has taken place in my forest home. Though I am loath to discover what I will find, I know that I must."

Gog stayed locked to Daniel until he was sure that the storm was truly on the wane, and then he left his bed and prepared to enter the twilight to assess whatever damage might have been left behind. He swiftly tucked the cat beneath the quilt where he would stay warm and protected. Then he covered Solomon's cage with his mother's shawl as he miserably huddled in his makeshift nest. Its additional warmth would provide comfort for the little bird until temperatures once again reflected summer's heat. The unusual cold, following this most ruthless of summer storms, made it necessary for Gog to stoke his fire and add a couple of large chunks of wood so that the cottage would regain its heat for the cool night to come.

After clapping his hat upon his head, slipping on a warm but shabby coat, and grabbing his walking stick—Gog slowly stepped out upon his doorstep and just stood there for a moment, trying to capture a sense of the changed environment with all his senses. They seemed to be heightened by the passing of the dramatic storm which was slow to leave the glen, charged by the vividness of the perceptions that they had left behind, and reeled with a sense of desolation in the wake of so much violence.

The ground was entirely saturated, and Gog's feet pressed deep into the soggy earth. Rivulets of rain water ran in desperation towards the brook, and the rain barrel groaned with the excess water that was held within. There was an unnatural silence now pervading the landscape, save for the patter of a few forlorn droplets of tardy rain. No birdsong and no wind. Huge puddles dotted the path through the woods, but Gog gingerly walked on, relying on his walking stick to prevent him from falling in the mire. He continued to shiver from the dire warnings that he felt—knowing without real proof that something terrible must have taken place just ahead.

"I do not believe myself to be an especially fearful gnome when it comes to something that I know little about. I don't normally flee from shadows or my own dark imaginings. But on this occasion, I do not look forward to traipsing through the darkening woods alone. My search for what will eventually be revealed to me at the end of my journey, something that has most likely forever been changed or destroyed by the catastrophic crashes that I heard, makes me quake with a bit of fear. I wonder if my world will ever be the same. My God is with me, and I remind myself, "Thy will be done."

Dread is a terrible burden on a soul, and Gog felt it this day. He had lived through many thunderstorms in his long life, but never one like this. The storm had penetrated his little forested glen, threatening it with destruction. His cottage, the plot of land around it, and the forest had always been his refuge—his *safety from the storm.* He shuddered to think that in one split second this harmful invasion had very nearly changed all that.

"I can't tell you why, but I truly think there will be a bad outcome to this day. I hesitate to go forward, fearing what it might mean to me and my little friends in the glade. The premature night seems so ominous. The wind has begun to moan again, and now a persistent drizzle has begun to fall upon the earth. Storm-tossed branches lie upon the ground, littering my path. The air is bitter with wet smoke, and the lightning continues to do battle in the distance. It is so dark and gloomy! Ominous rain clouds continue to scud across the sky, leaving little room for the light of the moon or the stars."

As Gog trudged on his way, in very measured footsteps, he was soon joined by Rogue, who silently materialized from the dense fog that was blanketing the earth. Gog felt much safer with his presence, for now he no longer felt so alone. The gnome and the fox traveled forward, hoping to locate what might have been destroyed or damaged by the fury of the storm.

The two travelers moved on in silence: looking, listening, and sniffing the air. Everything had been completely soaked by the passing storm. The moisture dripped loudly from the underbrush to the ground, and no other creatures seemed to be stirring. Evidently the mean-spirited rainstorm had sent them all scurrying for shelter, and they were not anxious to venture out so soon.

"I begin to sense that something is very, very wrong. I can feel it in my rapid pulse and in the noisy beating of my heart. Rogue's tread is soft but determined in the dark, and a low growl of warning keeps erupting from deep within him. He yips at an invisible enemy, though nothing of any substance crosses our path. The hackles rise on the back of his neck, and his eyes gleam an eerie yellow in the gloomy twilight. I cannot help but be terrified."

The two proceeded around the next bend, and then stopped—stock-still. They looked around in bewilderment, trying their best to determine what had changed within the landscape before them. Then Gog gasped in horror! His friend, Quaking Aspen, was shockingly absent. An ominous, empty space now gaped at the end of the path. A bare horizon loomed before them as far as the eye could see. Just a few large, straggly tree roots were lifted to the heavens, pointing upwards in misery from whence their destruction had come. Gog gulped air as he tried in vain to take in everything that was attacking his senses all at once.

"I cannot believe! I won't believe! This cannot be real! Perhaps I should go and come back, and the result of this day may change back to something else, something far more benign. Quaking Aspen! I must have taken a wrong turn! Perhaps Quaking Aspen is just around the bend."

Gog felt his tears begin to trickle from beneath his eyelids, and soon they were streaming down his cheeks. The gnome felt sick with the horror of the reality that he was now forced to face. "My poor friend! My poor, dear friend!"

The venerable old tree had been ferociously attacked by the raging thunderstorm, and he had crashed down across the forest path. The magnificent tree had met its end and had surrendered to the violent storm. Damaged beyond measure, it had finally collapsed to the earth from the relentless pull of gravity. Its once lush crown now lay scattered in disarray, and its blackened trunk blocked the path through the woodlands with the lost grandeur of its massive size. The forest floor before them was shrouded entirely by Gog's fallen comrade. A heartbreaking stillness pressed heavily upon this scene of death and destruction.

Quaking Aspen's very heart had been plundered by a sword of lightning that had splintered his every ring, laid waste to all but a few of his leaves, and viciously destroyed cords and cords of hardy fiber that had once soared up into the sky as tree trunk—sporting muscular branches that held bushels and bushels of greenery aloft. The tree's core, much of it hollow and ravaged by age, had not been able to withstand the vicious assault of the lightning, wind, and rain.

Quaking Aspen was now hardly recognizable as a tree, for he had been laid waste by the destructive forces of nature. One moment he had been standing tall and proud, waiting for the storm to complete its rampage; and then, within a matter of minutes, he had endured the deadly strike that had toppled him to the ground almost immediately so that he now lay sprawled upon the forest floor. Gog tried to take it all in, but he just could not.

“Gone! My friend Quaking Aspen is no more! With one wretched blow an ill-timed storm has destroyed him. How could this nightmare have ever happened to a tree so noble, so important to this world? How will I ever get over his loss?” Hot tears continued to glide down Gog’s weathered cheeks. A whimper escaped his lips.

“The many dreams I have dreamed while being held spellbound by the whispering of his leaves, the naps I have taken in the shade beneath his sheltering limbs, the messages I have attempted to decipher throughout the years to solve the mysteries of life—all are no more and will never be again. Nothing is left but my memories now.”

Gog began to shake with silent sobs. Rogue leaned against his leg, unusual as it was for the fox to welcome touch from another. The gnome gradually pulled himself together and then patted his friend. The two walked sadly around what was left of the aspen. Rogue growled at the simmering embers and wisps of smoke that still encircled the downed tree.

The poor gnome was totally conflicted and distressed about this precious world of his, which had just been dealt such a crushing blow. Though he totally trusted in his Father above to determine his fate along with the fate of the entire world, he also depended on Him now to answer his prayers as he sought guidance and protection for those he loved. How could he accept this punishment of loss and despair as a heavenly decree when all he could feel was pain and despair. Though his distress was great, he closed his eyes and gave himself up to the almighty will of his Maker, who in the end knew what was best—though his decree might not be necessarily understood or accepted by mortal beings.

Gog touched one of the tree's sprawling branches with reverence, "Quaking Aspen always stood steadfast while I sometimes complained about my fate. He murmured condolences when I grieved, and his rustling whispers encouraged me when I had problems I needed to solve. The soft breezes that rustled his leaves gave me hope when I despaired, and his limbs creaked in amusement when I was overcome by the joy of life. I could always count on this tree for its beauty, strength, listening powers, and wisdom. I will forever miss him."

With much sorrow, Gog paced the area around his downed friend, Rogue close at his heels. A gentle shower now filtered through the web of leaves that swayed above them. Rivulets of water snaked around the tree and doused the glowing embers. The wind blew away the remaining tendrils of smoke; and the air immediately cleared, though still smelling faintly of sulfur. The recent lightning strike was beginning to seem more and more like a bad dream. Drenched though they were, Gog and Rogue seemed in no hurry to leave their departed friend. This stretch of land now seemed mercilessly lonely and bereft of life.

"I will not be the only one to miss my lofty friend, Rogue. Many of his friends will mourn his passing. He has provided nesting sites for so many of the birds, trails for the chipmunks and squirrels, perches for the owl and the hawk, a message center for the ravens, and a feeding station for the woodpeckers. For the weary travelers he gave shade, shelter, and a haven from the storm. He mulched the forest floor with his leaves and filled the air with the pleasant sound of his rustling leaves. I just cannot imagine how we will ever adjust to the emptiness that he leaves behind." Gog took off his cap in reverence and solemnly knelt by the side of the downed aspen.

"I know that my friend will not want me to spend so much time on my grief that I forget to celebrate his long, full life. He will live on forever in the chronicles of this forest. These grounds will prove the resourcefulness of the earth where nothing goes to waste and transitions are but a necessity of life. Before I leave this hallowed spot, I must at least say a few words on behalf of my departed friend."

Quaking Aspen,
Remembered by all for years to come, he will leave a rich legacy,
returning to the rich forest floor from whence he came.
His toppled trunk will provide
shelters for the raccoon and dens for the fox.
His rotting limbs will provide
beetles for the skunk and grubs for the woodpecker.
His decaying limbs will provide
gardens for fungi and mushrooms.
His leaves and bark will provide
mulch for saplings and rich compost for ferns.
New saplings will compete to take his place,
but only Quaking Aspen will forever remain a legend of this forest.
Unforgettable friend—true sage—gentle soul of the woodlands.
You will continue to live on in our hearts and souls forever.

Gog chose a section of a limb that sported a large knot in the middle. The bark was untouched, and the cross-section where it had once joined the tree elaborated on its life with its circles of tree rings and marvelous grain. Gog would take this precious keepsake home to the cottage with him as a remembrance of his friend. He knew that the goodness that had once existed in his friend Quaking Aspen might somehow be captured in this new walking stick, and that the essence of his remarkable life and works would remain as a cherished keepsake forever. He knew without a doubt that he would always remember his friend and cherish all their memories for a lifetime.

Chapter 23
The Magnificent Hour

On the next day following the horrific storm, and still grieving the loss of Quaking Aspen, Gog ventured outside, hoping to capture a moment of peace and normalcy. He was immediately struck by the beauty of the morning, for the cottage was backlit by a rosy peach sunrise. The paths through the forest were still drenched by the passing storm and the early morning dew, but the grasses and foliage glittered brilliant green, the birds twittered in the trees, and a few butterflies flitted through the air. Though the landscape seemed slightly more subdued than usual, the gentle fragrance of rain and mint hung heavy in the air. This was not the ultimate devastation of his world that he had feared. The Lord's beneficence had scoured the land with a loving touch and left a gentle beauty behind.

Gog felt within his heart that the day must be Sunday, the Sabbath, though he really didn't know for sure. He never really did as he was tied more closely to the timeline of the land than to any formal calendar or timepiece. Somehow there seemed to be a solemnness and a rightness about the day—it *felt* like Sunday. As inaccurate as his celebrations of the Sabbath often were, they were still conducted with a certain solemnity and purity of soul. The hymns and prayers that the gnome offered from his heart were touching and sincere; and the blessings that fluttered down from on High would forgive him for the moral inaccuracies that might sometimes occur.

On this day especially, Gog felt that he needed to draw closer to God and his Son above to continue his prayers of the previous day concerning his lost friend, Quaking Aspen. He needed to give thanks for all those in the forest that had been spared devastation from the violent storm, which included himself, his friends, and his home. And he needed to show his appreciation for the beautiful day that had just recently dawned, a rebirth of sorts, reminding him of the many blessings he continually received from his Maker.

A small wooded hollow, not far from Selah's grave, had become Gog's outdoors chapel. It was a natural alcove of peaceful beauty that had been hollowed out of the earth by the forces of wind and rain, and the heavens had seen fit to decorate its perimeters with the plants, berries, trees, and flowers of each season. Whenever Gog approached the outdoor chapel, he routinely kneeled by Selah's grave for a morning prayer; and then he proceeded on to *church.*

The chapel itself was a small opening in the forest, which for some unknown reason was devoid of trees, shrubs, and vegetation. The forest floor clearing, though devoid of vegetation, had a scattering of leaves upon its surface. A well-worn stump was positioned here as a substitute for the gnome's personal pew, as was a moss-covered, flat rock that was frequently used as a kneeling bench for his prayer. The chapel's roof was a close formation of treetops that towered high above it, creating a natural steeple that rose to Heaven itself. The rustic church was, more-often-than-not, surrounded by the gentle hush of the woodlands and the gurgling of a nearby stream that trickled over the rocks in a nearby creek bed.

Due to the dense canopy, a minimum of dim lighting filtered down into the chapel. Occasionally a few stray sunbeams from Above interrupted the dark solemnity that hovered there. A large wooden cross, constructed of hand-hewn oaken beams lashed together with soft leather straps, was positioned at the front of the chapel. It was flanked by an abundance of forest ferns that bowed their fronds in respect, and this day purple geraniums bloomed to lend their beauty to this sacred place. This private house of prayer always stood ready to welcome and encourage the gnome's regular visitations. And though he was the only member there to bear witness, he was surrounded by the spirits of the forest who had once tread these very woods where he now bowed his head.

Today, especially, Gog felt that he owed it to God to visit and lay his life before him for His appraisal. For some reason, he felt that the upheaval caused by the storm the day before might have something to do with his seeking to address the sins within his own soul this day. He knew that it was important for him to be accessible to his Lord so that he could petition for his forever love, mercy, and forgiveness. He knew that he needed to seek some sense of heavenly comfort for the loss of Quaking Aspen and the devastation that took place in his woodlands. Perhaps the restlessness and anxiety that were plaguing his soul might find remedy here within this hallowed space.

Gog sat down upon his stump and tried to settle his thoughts with contemplation. He had so much on his mind, but he knew that he must empty it to allow for his Savior's entry. A small chipmunk scurried across the clearing, and the gnome was quickly shaken out of his reverie as he briefly tried to determine whether it could possibly be Martha. By the time he finally determined that it could not be, his utter disappointment sobered him, and he quickly bowed his head in prayer. For some reason, this day was beginning to feel very, very heavy. He needed his heavenly Father now more than ever, for the burdens of the world seemed to be far heavier than he could ever possibly manage by himself.

The gnome soon began to whisper *The Lord's Prayer.* It was a comforting prayer that seemed to acknowledge, beckon, and welcome his Maker all at once. Gog waited for the silence, his prayers, and the hunger in his soul to work their magic. He was soon answered by a golden sunbeam that slanted down through the foliage, resting upon the prayer bench—inviting him to take his place there. As he kneeled there in an attitude of prayer, the sunbeam enveloped him in its beautiful, celestial light; and its presence turned the gnome's thoughts to his need for redemption, thanksgiving, and charity. He no longer felt alone. He felt loved, comforted, and forgiven for his sins. And his heavy heart seemed to have found wings. What a blessing!

I am not alone. I have never ever been truly alone. I should never allow my doubts to shadow my life with a darkness of spirit that prevents me from seeking the joys that the good Lord above so freely provides—but I do. I should not question my purpose or worry about a future I cannot see when the good Lord above has already made plans for me—yet I do. Why must I constantly number the world's many heavy troubles when the good Lord above has provided me with so many wonderful blessings that need to be counted instead? I am but a lonely gnome who sometimes stumbles as I go, but I do indeed seriously focus on the Light ahead, which is my hope beyond this life.

"Dear Lord in heaven, please hear my prayers this day as I try to heed your many lessons. Your love always surrounds me, that I know; and You constantly forgive me for my many sins. You shoulder so many of my earthly burdens, and yet You are seldom repaid with the undying gratitude that You deserve. I know that there are times when I try to avoid You as I attempt to hide from both You and Your dictates."

"I do not always accept my responsibilities as a true believer. I often fail to realize that sorrow is but the opposite dimension of joy, and both must necessarily exist together on this earth. This world is not a perfect world, and never shall it be—for it is but a fleeting mortal world that does no more than prepare us for eternity. Thank You for Your constant presence and love eternal, God. May I go forward from this place with renewed hope and purpose, and may I continue to do good works that are pleasing to You. May I strive to become more selfless, compassionate, and loving. May I be less critical, selfish, and worldly. Thank you for hearing my prayers, dear Lord. Amen."

The peace that exceeded all worldly expectations was found by Gog in the little woodland chapel that day, and it was the kind of peace for which men's souls often ache. It whispered of a love that is found when heartache is finally abandoned, of the sweet surrender that is made to a heavenly Father who but waits for His love to be reciprocated, and of the type of joy that does not rely on the material treasures of this earth but on selfless compassion. The time for worship, which Gog had carved out for himself within the course of his life, day by day, and hour by hour, was an affirmation of his faith.

Today's worship was special. There had been a holiness about it that he had not always been witness to on his previous visits. He felt that God had drawn closer to him, as if to impart special instruction, or perhaps celestial recommendations that needed to be addressed in the coming days. He had felt his soul expand and had even sensed that an understanding of what his life had been and what it needed to be might be almost within his grasp. His soul stirred to life and his heart grew to its very limits it seemed. It had been *the most magnificent hour*.

Chapter 24
A Season Of Change

Spring was finally making its rounds again, and all those who had awakened to the radiant sunrise and gentle breezes were celebrating its return. A red-wing black bird was trilling his full-throated song. A mother Canada goose was walking her goslings from their nest to the gurgling brook in the swamp for the first time. Rogue had vacated his den two weeks past; he now wore the brilliant red mantle of an adult fox and was intent upon finding a mate. Change was in the air.

Gog sat on his stoop, weaving a basket from willow wands and marsh reeds. He would soon collect his first harvest of fiddleheads, wild onions, and dandelion greens. His old basket had weakened with the many years of use. It had been woven by his mother many years ago, but he had been forced to reluctantly feed it to the fire this day when the bottom had fallen out. Now he needed to create a new one for the long season of gathering that stretched before him.

The cottage door hung loosely on its hinges. It had swung open, allowing the fragrant spring breezes and the golden sunshine to enter Gog's home. The breezes played around Solomon's cage and fluttered the curtains at the lonely window. The sun slanted through the window and came to rest upon the rough-hewn table in the center of the room. A homely tablecloth was spread, and upon it rested a bouquet of cowslips, a loaf of seeded bread, and a sleeping cat.

Daniel had been told time and time again that he did not belong there on the table, especially as he had reached adulthood.

However, the cat viewed the table as a substantial *perch*, which would allow him a wonderful view of the surrounding cottage floor and doorway—as he was always vigilant to the scurry of mouse's feet and the visit of some unsuspecting rabbit that he might spy through the open door, and so he persisted.

The green bottle containing Selah vibrated with its other-worldly green light at the furthest end of the table—sitting at rest in its revered location. Flies buzzed drowsily upon the windowsill. A stew of mushrooms, fiddleheads, and wild onion simmered in a cauldron. Gentle breezes soughed through the trees, and for a time peace reigned.

Daniel softly purred as he dozed in the sunshine, his whiskers twitching from time to time as his slumber deepened. He was enjoying a pleasant dream that seemed far too lifelike to be but mere fantasy. In his dream he was pursuing an especially plump little mouse, and it was becoming evident that he was only moments away from capturing his meal. He was getting closer and closer to the mouse, and success seemed almost imminent. His dream pattern was quickly beginning to quicken, however, and his body prepared for a final, dramatic pounce. The excitement generated by this adventure was quickly being transmitted to his claws, his nails unsheathing in preparation for the hunt. Gog, sitting by the hearth, was totally oblivious to Daniel and his dream, and could not predict that Daniel's pleasant dream might very well become his very own worst nightmare.

Daniel was winning the race with the phantom mouse, and his mouth salivated with the expectancy of a succulent dinner. With one last burst of speed, and a quick jerk of his body, he quickly closed in on his target. He awoke with a start, just as his right paw swept the glass bottle containing Selah's soul smashing to the floor. The bottle struck the stone hearth and shattered into pieces in an instant.

Daniel's eyes immediately narrowed into slits. Realizing that what he had done was BAD, he quickly leapt to the floor and ran out through the open doorway—quickly melting into the glade beyond. If a cat had the ability to feel remorse, Daniel felt it now; and he fled far beyond Gog's reach because he did not want to face his wrath for the sorry deed for which he was responsible.

At the sound of the crash, Gog immediately jumped up in horror. He rushed to the table at the very same moment that Daniel rushed out the door of the cottage. He stared in disbelief at the glowing essence of his mother as it hovered above the shards of glass upon the floor. Feeling helpless, and terrified of his impending loss, he frantically tried to find another container with which he might recapture the wayward soul before it had the chance to escape. The green mist throbbed with the pulse of life, and its light source sparkled and glowed with the freedom it had found beyond the bottle.

Gog was frantic and in shock. No container could easily be found. His mother's presence was now waning as he stood by in dismayed silence. He trembled in awe as he watched his mother's spirit lift heavenward and then hover above the table. The gnome had truly expected that her spirit when released would immediately dissipate, yet still it lingered. For some reason, it seemed almost reluctant to take advantage of the catastrophe that had freed it. Something seemed to be holding it back—at least for the moment.

"Though I feel like I am dying on the inside from what I thought would be a huge loss, I begin to sense that true heartbreak might not take place upon this occasion. For some reason I can feel the guilt that I have carried around with me for these many years easing— it seems to be releasing its hold on me. I begin to feel the stirrings of a real sense of joy welling up from deep inside, and I begin to wonder why that might be.

Selah's spirit seems to be showering me with the radiance of her love and forgiveness. My heart truly swells with these gifts that stream from my mother to me, her son."

In a shiny moment of overwhelming joy, the gnome had the most magnificent epiphany: an epiphany that constricted his breathing and came close to bursting his heart. Gog somehow *knew* that the throbbing soul of Selah, which had just been given unconditional freedom to soar to the gates of Heaven, God's home, was hesitant to leave him. She had remained there because she chose to. There was unfinished business between the two of them that still demanded resolution.

"I know my mother is praying for me to wish her *Godspeed*— to send her on her way with both my permission and my undying love. It is a final gift that I certainly do not wish to deny her. She has always given me her everything, and it is now my turn to give back. Still—I die a little bit when I think of her leaving me totally alone."

However, Gog's love for her swelled within him, and he felt compelled to bring a sense of closure to her impending departure. He knew that it was past time, and that Selah's soul had never deserved to be imprisoned. It must now become free, prepared after all this time for its final journey, and accompanied with all the love and well wishes that Gog could send with it.

"As I watch the spirit of my mother, I know that what I see is really her; but it is also so much more. The pulsing green light that flickers and throbs is colored with eternity, tinged with joy, and infused with a forever love. It speaks of grace, and patience, and kindness. And I realize that her presence for the many long hours, days, weeks, and years had all been totally sacrificial on her part. She had not been forced to stay with me in the cottage, she had chosen to stay with me. She had sacrificed her soul that belonged with God for her only child. I feel very much the sinner for having robbed her of her eternity until this moment."

Gog hung his head, feeling ashamed at the meanness of his own spirit—a spirit that had once sought the imprisonment of his mother's precious soul for his own selfish reasons. He knew that the pain of his impending loneliness had not been justification for denying her soul its freedom. He had sinned, and yet his mother had selflessly chosen to remain within the bottle in which he had imprisoned her if it would bring him a bit of comfort and staunch his grief.

"I should have known then, as I know now, that a spirit, the very living soul, is something that may never be captured or contained by any mortal being—for it is no longer of this world. It belongs to the larger, Light-filled world that beckons from beyond. It is celestial and remains in limbo only until it can finally reconnect and become one with God. How wrong I was!"

"I am no more than what I am—a woodland gnome. I have never possessed the power to prevent my mother from leaving me. Selah had chosen to stay of her own accord, providing me what comfort she could in my time of loss. She gave unselfishly of her mother's love at the very time her soul strove completion and freedom in Heaven. I was so very selfish, and she was so very brave and giving. I must forever ask God and Jesus to forgive me for this sin. Sorrow and loneliness were poor excuses for my deed; nonetheless, I had set out to deprive my mother of her place in God's mansion. In trying to prevent her final, magnificent homecoming—I had been sinful." He clasped his hands in front of him and thought about his mother's sacrifice. He prayed to his Savior to give him the strength and determination to do what was right.

Gog now felt the conflict of pain and exhilaration in the recognition of what his mother's soul had been striving for: pain that his mother had deferred her soul's heavenly completion for him, and exhilaration in knowing that her soul was finally freed to leave the earthly world and soar towards Heaven as he finally gave her a son's blessing. The splendor of eternity awaited her with God's boundless love. She would live forever in a kingdom that had been prepared for her long ago, and there she would patiently wait for her son to join her.

Gog knew that his life was about to irrevocably change, and that what he had once accepted as a way of life, would soon be no more. His mother was about to depart this world and leave her son behind, and he would not know when he might expect to be reunited with her again. However, as he prepared himself for her leave-taking, he felt the miraculous stirrings of hope within his own soul.

"The beautiful butterfly does indeed emerge from its homely cocoon! Metamorphosis. It does exist! I was right in believing it so. It is not something that is reserved for just a few, but it is possible for all. I have been so selfish and stubborn in trying to keep Selah by my side when she should have become the most beautiful of all butterflies long ago. Her spirit belongs with the sunbeams and the moonbeams, with eternal love, with God and Jesus. My mother's love was the only thing that prevented her from continuing her journey home, and I was the cause for her lingering here on earth. I feel so much shame for my part in delaying her journey. God has so many lessons yet for me to learn."

The flickering green light closed the space between the rafters and the table and was now hovering close to Gog. The gnome gently cupped this remaining radiance within his coarse and knobby hands, and he gazed upon it in reverence. His voice was soft and pure as he recited what would be his final poem to his mother:

A mother's love is soft and pure,
precious as the golden spring—
Where songbirds raise their voices in chorus,
Wildflowers bloom in gay profusion,
And gentle winds blow white clouds aloft.
Nothing this fragile may remain on earth forever,
For eternity awaits the angel that will one day wing her way
From a mother's broken heart to Heaven
Where she will finally seek eternal peace with God.

Selah knew that Gog was reluctant but ready to wish her *Godspeed*, and that his final, loving farewell would send her on her final journey at last. Her essence warmed and trembled in Gog's hand as their bittersweet emotions exemplified the love they shared with one another. Finally, she heard what she had longed to hear for the many years that had passed.

"My sweet mother, I must say good-bye to you now, wishing you *Godspeed.* Though you leave me, you will not go alone, for all my love and devotion will go with you on your journey. Please remember me with love and forgiveness until the day when the two of us meet once more, never to be separated again. May God's will be done, and our Savior's love surround you."

Selah's light glowed with just a bit more brilliance; but she could delay her journey no longer. Her soul gradually rose above her son where it hovered for a time but inches from the rafters, reluctant to bestow its final farewell. Then it gradually dissipated amongst the mote-flecked sunbeams until it was no more. A shimmer of gold drifted above the table for the briefest of moments, and then it too disappeared as if it had never been.

The gnome bowed his head in silence and prayer as he was overcome by the conflicting emotions of elation, sorrow, and relief. He felt totally spent, drained, and empty. But, ironically, he also felt totally full—brimming with love, peace, and joy. He felt forgiven. Gog sought his rocking chair and wrapped himself in his mother's old shawl, which still possessed a decades-old whiff of her fragrance and a few strands of her silvery hair. The early spring day was still gentle and warm, but he suddenly felt a chill that no amount of sunshine could erase.

For Gog it was as if a huge weight had been finally lifted from his shoulders, and he slumped a bit in the chair. "I have finally accepted the loss of my mother and wished her *Godspeed.* She now journeys to her destiny with all my heartfelt blessings. My good wishes for her departure were long overdue, and I can only pray that God will forgive me and continue to bless me and my humble life until the day when he prepares a place for me in His heavenly home where my mother now resides."

***

Time would go on for Gog in his little cottage in the woods. He would not rush death, for his lungs still filled with the preciousness of life. He embraced the beauty and mysteries of life. And he knew that his Maker would chart his life's journey as He always had, and that when his time came God would bring him home to Heaven. He knew that his soul would be ready, and its wings would beat joyously to Heaven where his heavenly Father and his mother awaited him.

— The End —

www.ingramcontent.com/pod-product-compliance
Lightning Source LLC
Chambersburg PA
CBHW070629310726
48982CB00001B/220

* 9 7 8 1 9 7 0 3 7 9 2 8 0 *